"HELP! WATCH IT!" THOMAS J YELLED SUDDENLY.

He grabbed my arm and yanked hard. "Run! They're alive."

I looked where he was looking. Bees, a million bees! They were swarming toward us from out of the hive, zillions of them, a whole black cloud of them.

"They're after us!" Thomas J yelled. He looked around wildly.

At that exact moment I saw my ring.

I reached for it just as the black cloud zoomed at my head.

Forget the ring!

"Run!" I shouted to Thomas J. "Run for your life!"

I jumped to my feet, and he did, too.

I raced for the water, the bees right above my head. "In the water!" I shouted. "In the lake."

"But I got my clothes on!" Thomas J shouted. He stopped at the edge of the water.

I didn't care what he did. I didn't stop to argue, either.

I just threw myself into the lake, clothes and shoes and all.

In just a second Thomas J splashed in next to me. . . .

Books by Patricia Hermes

BE STILL MY HEART
MY GIRL

Available from ARCHWAY Paperbacks

HEADS, I WIN
KEVIN CORBETT EATS FLIES

Available from MINSTREL® Books

MY GIRL

A novel by Patricia Hermes
based on the motion picture
written by Laurice Elehwany

AN ARCHWAY PAPERBACK
Published by POCKET BOOKS
New York   London   Toronto   Sydney   Tokyo   Singapore

AN ARCHWAY PAPERBACK *Original*

An Archway Paperback published by
POCKET BOOKS, a division of Simon & Schuster Inc.
1230 Avenue of the Americas, New York, NY 10020

ISBN: 0-671-75929-9

First Archway Paperback printing December 1991

10 9 8 7 6 5 4 3 2 1

AN ARCHWAY PAPERBACK and colophon are registered
trademarks of Simon & Schuster Inc.

Printed in the U.S.A.

IL 6+

For My Boys: Paul, Mark, Tim and Matthew
And My Girl: Jennifer

—P. H.

MY GIRL

I was born jaundiced. Once I was in a bathroom at a truck stop and caught hemorrhoids. And I've learned to live with the chicken bone that's been stuck in my throat ever since Gramoo got sick—well, mostly I've learned. Although I was getting more worried about it lately, because I could feel it getting bigger.

I've also learned to live with the dead people we always have in the basement and the living room. And that's true—there really *are* dead people here. They bring them to the basement, and then, when they're finished with them there, they dress them up and put them in the living room. Harry J. Sultenfuss, Parlor, it says on the brass plate outside our door. What it means is funeral parlor. That's my home.

It's creepy being surrounded by dead people all the time—dead people and others who are crying over the dead ones. I wondered if Dad cried a lot when my mother died. I don't remember it of course, because she died when I was born. But I try not to think about that.

So it's just me and my dad. Dad likes me okay enough, I guess, but he has problems talking about it. I guess lots of dads have trouble talking to their daughters. At least, that's what Gramoo says—what Gramoo used to say before she got weird and stopped talking.

Anyway, with all that's happened and that I've had to learn to live with, I figured Dad would be upset about my latest affliction—this chicken bone stuck in my throat and the lump that was growing up around it. I had to tell him. This was serious.

We were in the kitchen together, and Dad was at the counter by the window, making a sandwich. He was frowning down at it like it was some puzzle to figure out.

"Dad," I said.

He didn't answer.

"Dad?" I said louder.

He still didn't answer.

"Hey, Dad!"

"Hmmm?" he said, but he didn't look up from his sandwich.

"I don't want to upset you," I said, "but you know this thing in my throat? I think it's getting bigger. I can't swallow well. I think it's cancer maybe. You think I'm dying?"

"Hand me the mayonnaise out of the fridge, would you, Vada?" he said.

He couldn't hear me, that's what it was. I wasn't

2

making any sound. Maybe I was invisible, too? Add that to the cancer and the hemorrhoids.

I got the mayonnaise and brought it to him.

He said, "Thanks, Vada," but he didn't look up or anything.

Maybe you get invisible from living around dead people?

I sighed and went out on the porch. Thomas J was coming over in a little while. I could talk to him about it. I tell him practically everything. I even told him I was in love with Mr. Bixler, our fifth grade teacher this past year.

I wished I could talk to Gramoo about it. Once I could have told her, but for the last few months she acts like everyone is invisible, not just me. It's like the only real people are the ones she sees inside her head, people she sings to—sometimes at the top of her lungs—but that no one else sees.

I sat on the porch and looked at my watch. Thomas J was late.

But just as I was convinced he wasn't coming, I saw him. He was heading for my house on his bike, and about a block behind him were some other kids on bikes, calling to him and yelling. From here I couldn't hear what they were saying, but I knew they were tormenting him. Thomas J is so easy to torment— what with him being allergic to everything and skinny and scared of so many things—that practically every- one in Mr. Bixler's class this year teased him, even me. But I'm not mean the way I do it. I like Thomas J. He's my best friend, has been ever since Gramoo and Thomas J's mother, Mrs. Sennett, met at the playground with me and Thomas J when we were two years old.

Thomas J skidded to a stop in front of me. His glasses slid down his nose, and he punched at them with one finger. There was tape around them holding them together.

"If you punch them any more," I said, "they're going to split in a million pieces."

"Vada!" he said. He turned and looked nervously over his shoulder, down the block to where the others were, then turned back to me. "Is it true that you're showing them one? A *body?*"

"Who?"

"Howie and Billy?"

"Uh-oh," I said. I'd forgotten. A week ago, on the last day of school, some of them were teasing me about being best friends with Thomas J, teasing and saying he was a big baby and all. So I told them they wouldn't be nearly as brave as him, that they wouldn't come in and see a corpse. And then when they said they would, I said they'd have to pay to see one.

Of course, they didn't have to know that Thomas J had never seen one either, that he'd never even been in my house once in all the years we'd been friends.

"Are you?" Thomas J said now.

I nodded. "If they pay up."

"But how come?" Thomas J said.

"How come what?"

"How come you're showing them?"

I just shrugged. I wasn't going to tell him that they'd been making fun of him. So I just said, "Why not?"

4

Howie and Billy came up then and dropped their bikes to the grass.

"So? Gonna show us?" Howie asked.

"Yeah, are you?" Billy said.

"Got your money?" I said to them all. "Who's in?"

They raised their hands, all but Thomas J.

Howie and Billy dug in their pockets.

Eventually Howie handed me fifty cents.

Thomas J was backing up.

"You coming or not, Thomas J?" Howie said.

"Nah," I said, "he's seen plenty of them. He's tired of them, right, Thomas J?"

"Can't," Thomas J said. "I hafta go home."

"To play with your dolls?" Billy said.

"Let him alone!" I said. "And where's your money? You didn't pay up."

"How do we know you're going to show us any?" he said.

"Talk about a baby!" I said. "You want it in writing so your mom can sign it?"

He glared at me, but after a minute, he said, "All right, all right."

He handed me a quarter.

I kept my hand out.

He sighed, then handed me another.

"Finally!" I said. "Now follow me. And don't say a single word."

I turned and saw Thomas J pedaling down the street alone. He'd be back later, after lunch, I knew.

I went up the steps to the porch, the two of them following. I was madly trying to come up with a plan, because I didn't think we had any dead bodies there right then—none except maybe a new one in the basement where Dad worked on them. And I sure wasn't going down there.

But then suddenly I had an idea, a plan so good it almost made me laugh out loud.

Very quietly we went into the house and I led them to a big room off the hall in the front of the house. We live in the back part of the house, but the rooms where the dead people are and the offices and all, those are in the front. I slid open a door and motioned them to come into the casket showroom. They didn't know it was just a showroom, though.

They followed me in, and I closed the door behind us.

There were lots of caskets in there, some open, some closed.

On tiptoe, I went over to a closed casket, the two boys following.

I put both my hands on the lid and stood there for a long time, just looking down at it, not saying a word.

"What are we waiting for?" Howie whispered. His voice came out all quivery, sort of.

"Giving you a chance to leave if you want," I answered.

Nobody moved.

"No one is chicken?" I said.

"Not me!" Billy said. But I thought he sounded kind of quivery, too.

Very solemnly then I turned to them. "You sure about this? You want to go through with this, both of you?"

6

Nobody spoke for a minute. And then Billy said, "Go ahead!"

"Okay, then," I said, "if you're sure."

I turned back to the coffin then, put both hands on it, and said softly, "All right. Lean forward."

They did.

"Ready?" I said.

They nodded.

Quickly then I flipped open the top half of the casket.

Nothing! There was nothing in there at all.

They squealed and jumped back.

Billy squealed the loudest.

I felt like laughing out loud. But I didn't. Instead, I frowned, putting on my most serious look.

"Uh-oh!" I said. I dropped the lid and put my hand to my mouth. "I was afraid of this."

"Of what?" Billy said.

"What?" Howie asked.

"It's this problem we have," I said softly. "See, sometimes when we get these people, they're not completely dead. You know, like when you cut a chicken's head off and they still run around crazy?"

"You're full of it," Billy said, but his voice was definitely shaky now.

"It was an old lady," I whispered. "She was so old she just stopped breathing one day. But maybe she started up again. I bet she's roaming around this house right now. Come on. Let's see if we can find her. Follow me."

I tiptoed to the door, then peeked out into the hall. No one was around.

Very carefully I slid open the door, and all of us went out and I quietly closed it behind us.

Then I led the way down the hall to our part of the house in the back.

Being careful to be super quiet, and hoping and praying she was there, I opened the door to our kitchen–family room. I peeked in.

There she was—Gramoo—just as I had hoped. She was sitting motionless in her rocker, bolt upright, absolutely still, her veined hands clutching the armrests. She was so still that for a minute even I could imagine that she was dead.

I looked over my shoulder at Howie and Billy.

They were staring at Gramoo, bugged-eyed, hardly breathing. Something in Billy's throat was bobbing up and down, and he was so white I was sure he'd faint.

"That's her," I whispered. "I knew it."

I turned back to Gramoo.

She just kept sitting there, still, stiff as a dead person, the way she does most all the time now.

But then as we watched, suddenly she began to rock.

There was this stifled, choking cry behind me. And when I turned, they were running down the hall and out the front door.

Laughing, I watched them go. I tucked my hands under my arms and flapped my elbows. "Bock, bock, bock!" I squawked.

See if they made fun of Thomas J for being a chicken again!

I went over to Gramoo then. I bet she'd love to know how she'd scared them. A couple months ago she'd have laughed a lot about this.

"Hi, Gramoo!" I said. "You scared them good. Boy, did you."

She didn't answer.

"Gramoo?"

I knelt in front of her, looking up into her face.

She didn't see me. Or if she did, she didn't show it.

I miss her so much. She's like my mom. For years I even thought she *was* my mom, until I grew up and knew more. So what had happened to her? How could she be here but *not* be here? If only she'd try. She used to hold me and pat me, and when I got scared or anything, she'd sing to me and rock me in her lap, right in this rocker.

Suddenly I had a weird thought. I looked around, just to be sure no one was watching. Then, like a little kid, I climbed into her lap, curling myself into a little ball, just like I used to do when I was little.

"Gramoo?" I whispered.

She didn't notice me even then. Her face was as blank as a sleeping baby's.

"Gramoo?" I whispered. "Can you see me? Do you know it's me sitting here?"

She just rocked on.

"Please?" I whispered, and I put a hand on her hair and stroked it softly. "Try," I said. "Come on, Gramoo. Try? You can talk if you try."

*T*here was no answer from Gramoo, but Dad was calling me—loud.

Uh-oh! He'd found out we'd been playing in the casket room.

Slowly I got up off Gramoo's lap, then patted her hair once more. "Be right back," I whispered. "You stay there and I'll come back."

"Vada?" Dad called again.

"Coming!" I yelled back.

"Vada!" Dad yelled. "Would you bring my cigarettes down?"

Down. Down where he worked on dead people.

But at least it wasn't to yell at me about what I'd been doing.

I picked up the cigarettes from the counter. Then I went to the basement door. It was stuck, like always. I wiggled and pushed and finally opened it. Then I went slowly down the steps. But I stopped on the bottom step. I never step off the bottom step.

Dad was standing at the counter, his back to me, working on a body that was hooked up to an embalming machine. I tried not to look, but even though it was gross, I peeked. I always had to peek when I came down here.

Yuck.

Uncle Phil was helping. Uncle Phil works part-time for Dad, helping with all the gross stuff, like embalming and picking up bodies from hospitals and morgues. The other part of the time he's a bartender. They were really engrossed in what they were doing, and neither of them had heard me come down.

I didn't want to speak and scare them. I mean, they *were* working on a dead person.

So I coughed—a small, delicate sound.

"Phil," Dad said, "move him a few inches to your left, will you?"

Uncle Phil moved the body, and Dad checked the machine.

"Did I tell you he was my shop teacher?" Dad said.

"You took shop?" Uncle Phil said.

"Yep. I made a tie rack."

"No kidding!" Uncle Phil said. *"I* made a tie rack. And bookends, too."

I coughed again.

"Put them on the counter, Vada," Dad said, still not looking up.

And come off the step? No way.

I flipped them—a quick twist of the wrist and then—*swish!* Two points. Like a pro. I knew I'd make it as a basketball star someday. They landed right beside Dad on the counter.

"Daddy?" I said. "Guess what? I beat Thomas J in Monopoly yesterday."

For a minute Dad didn't say anything. And then he said, "Holds six ties. I still have it."

"Uncle Phil!" I said.

"Va-ta!" he answered.

"I beat Thomas J in Monopoly yesterday."

"Good for you, baby," Uncle Phil said.

"Once you put the hotels on Boardwalk and Park Place, you're a shoo-in to win," I told him.

"I like to buy up the railroads," Uncle Phil answered.

"We're trying to work here, Vada," Dad said.

"Daddy," I said. "Thomas J's mother took us to see *101 Dalmatians*. Cruella De Ville stole all the puppies. She was going to make a fur out of them."

"Phil, check the carotid artery, will you?" Dad said.

I sat down on the step, waiting. Maybe they'd be finished soon.

I tapped my fingers on the steps. " 'Doo wah diddy, diddy dum, diddy doo,' " I sang quietly.

Gramoo always says—said—I have a pretty voice.

"Vada!" Dad said.

"Dad?"

"Vada, I'm embalming my high school teacher. Don't sing."

I stood up. There was a clipboard against the wall by the steps and I picked it up and looked at it.

"Layton, Charles," it said. "Age 60. Cancer of the larynx."

Larynx! That was your throat, wasn't it?

He was dead. And he had the same thing I did—a lump in his throat. Maybe it wasn't a chicken bone. Maybe it really *was* cancer!

I started back upstairs. As soon as Thomas J got back here, we'd go see Dr. Welty.

I was halfway up the stairs when the doorbell rang.

Thomas J!

But when I opened the door, it wasn't Thomas J at all. It was a lady—a very fancy-looking lady. Right away I realized that she wasn't what Gramoo would have called a "real lady," back when Gramoo was still talking. This lady had on tons of makeup, and her eyelids were smudged with so much dark stuff she looked like she'd been punched, and her earrings hung down to her shoulders practically.

Her hair was frizzed out all over, and her dress was cut so low you could see practically all the way down the front of it.

Wow!

"Is Mr. Harry Sultenfuss in?" she asked.

"That's my father."

"Could I talk to him?"

"Sure," I said. I opened the door wider, and she came in.

"So," I said, once she was in the hall, "have you had the unfortunate experience of recently losing a loved one?"

She blinked at me. "Excuse me?" she said.

"Have you had the unfortunate—"

"Could I see your dad for just a second?" she said.

13

I went to the basement door and yelled down, "Dad! Somebody's here!"

"I'll be right up," he answered.

I came back to her. "He's downstairs," I said, "working on Mr. Layton. Throat cancer. Once it hits your throat, you're a goner. Can't talk or eat. So they just starve to death. At least the men do."

"Oh?" she said. She looked around, a little wild looking, I thought.

Dad opened the basement door, still slipping into his jacket. When he saw the lady, he came over to her, a serious look on his face, this I'm-so-sorry-for-your-troubles look that he gives out a lot. To strangers.

"How may I help you?" he said.

"I'm Shelly De Voto," she said. "I called the other day about the makeup artist job? It's still available, I hope."

"Oh, yes," Dad said. But then I saw him look her over, from her long, dangly earrings down to her high, high heels. "I think it's available," he added.

Right away I could see that she knew what he was thinking, same as me. She whipped this paper out of her purse. "Look!" she said. "See? I'm a licensed cosmetologist. I went to the Roosevelt College of Cosmetic Arts and graduated first in a class of twenty. I worked for two years at the Dino Raphael Salon, and my customers cried when I told them I was leaving. And I—"

"Miss De Voto," Dad interrupted.

". . . have a very good disposition!" she continued, like he hadn't even spoken. "I put people at ease and—"

"Miss De Voto!" Dad said, loud enough to stop her. "Miss De Voto, these people are already at ease." He paused. "This is not a beauty parlor. It's a funeral parlor."

Shelly looked from Dad to me, then back again. "They're dead?" she said finally.

Both Dad and I nodded.

"Yes, they are," Dad said.

"You're kidding!" she said. *"Stiffs?"*

I laughed right out loud.

Dad frowned at me. "Deceased!" he said.

"Wow!" Shelly shook her head. "And to think . . . The ad just said makeup artist."

Suddenly she started to laugh. "You mean that I drove all night and ended up in a funeral parlor?"

Dad and I both nodded again.

"Wow!" she said again.

She and Dad were just staring at each other.

I didn't think that was getting us anywhere.

I went and looked out through the front door.

A van and a camper were parked out front. Two men were getting out of the van and coming up to the house. They were carrying coffins—small coffins, smaller than I've ever seen before.

I opened the door as they came up on the porch.

Dad turned and saw them. "Hi, George," he said. "Be right back," he said to Shelly and me. And he went with the men to the casket display room.

I stayed at the door looking out.

"Is that your camper?" I asked Shelly.

"Yes, it is," Shelly said.

"Do you live in it?"

"Yes, yes, I do." And then she added, "A funeral home. Who would've thought?"

"How do you go to the bathroom?" I asked.

"What!" she said.

"In your camper."

"Oh. There's one in it."

"That's really cool."

Dad and the men came out of the display room, and the men went back to the van.

"Daddy?" I said when they were gone. "Why are those coffins so small? Are they for kids?"

For a minute Dad didn't answer. And then he said, "Of course not."

"Why are they so small, then?"

"They come in all sizes," Dad said. "Like shoes."

"Dad!" I put my hands on my hips. "Dad, are they for children?"

"I told you. No."

"Who are they for, then?"

Dad looked away. "Short people," he said after a minute. "Very short people."

I didn't believe him.

I looked at Shelly. She was nervous. She didn't believe him, either, I could tell. She swallowed hard. "What about the job?"

Dad's eyebrows went up. "You still want it? Even though—"

"Sure! Look, it's not a big deal because . . . because . . ."

I could practically see her mind working, moving fast the way mine did when I had to make up an excuse in school. Boy, she must really need the money, I thought.

". . . because, well, you see," she went on, "all my former clients will eventually die. And all yours used to be alive. So they have something in common!"

She smiled, real pleased with herself.

Made sense to me.

But Dad was still looking her over, still doubtful-looking, thinking about her makeup and stuff, I bet.

"So," she added, "I could still use all my same skills!"

"Except for the good disposition part," I said.

"You'd be doing hair and makeup and answering the phone," Dad said.

"And the salary?" Shelly asked.

"A hundred dollars."

"A week?"

Dad nodded.

Wow! I'd like a hundred a week. But not this job, this job I wouldn't do for a thousand a week.

"This is like a bad dream," Shelly said, rubbing her fingers over her forehead. "Look, I was hoping for about one-fifty. A hundred is less than what I made at my last job. And those customers tipped."

I could tell Dad was thinking about that.

"I can do a hundred and ten," he said finally.

She stuck out her hand. "Mr. Sultenfuss, you have a deal."

Dad took her hand, but just for a second. "You can start now," he said. "And I'm Harry." He looked her over. "Is that what you wear to work?" he asked.

"No," she said. "This is my interview suit. Look, I promise I'll take good care of these people. They deserve it. I mean, they're dead. All they got left is their looks." She paused. "I almost forgot, here are some of my references."

She pulled some papers out of her purse, and as she handed them to Dad, she dropped them all over the floor.

She and Dad both went to pick them up at the same time.

As he and Shelly were straightening up, I noticed that Dad noticed what I'd noticed before—that you could see practically all the way down Shelly's dress.

Dad shook his head at me.

I smiled back.

CHAPTER

III

*D*ad and Shelly went into Dad's office to do "paper-work," Dad called it.

I went outside. Thomas J hadn't come back, so I decided I'd go call for him. But when I went out, I didn't have to go find him. He was by the side of the house, sitting on the lawn beside his bike, pulling up bits of grass and sprinkling them on his legs, waiting for me like he was my pet dog or something.

"Come on, Thomas J," I said. "Let's go."

"To the willow tree?" Thomas J said.

"No," I said. "We have to see Dr. Welty. Come on."

But he didn't move. "Why?" he said. "Something new happen?"

I didn't answer. My throat was hurting something awful.

"Come on," I said. "Please. You know I need you with me."

He nodded. "Okay," he said.

We hopped on our bikes and went around the corner to Dr. Welty's.

Inside, there was no one in the waiting room, just Mrs. Randall, his nurse, at the desk.

"Well, hello, Miss Vada. Thomas J." She nodded. "And what's wrong with you today, missy?" she said to me.

She emphasized "today" like she saw me every day or something.

And she *doesn't* see me every day. Maybe a lot, but not every day.

"I'm very sick," I said, ignoring her mean comment.

She sighed. "Take a seat. I'll see if Dr. Welty has time to see you.

She left, and in a minute she was back out. "Okay, missy. Room number two. Your usual."

I went in. As I passed examining room one, I saw a kid in a wheelchair—a wheelchair! And a little kid, too. He must be really sick. Was he going to die? Was one of those short coffins for him?

My throat hurt even more.

I climbed up on the examining table just as Dr. Welty came in. Dr. Welty is old—really old, with lots of white hair and a kind of wrinkled up face. But he walks real fast, like he's lots younger. And he's always nice to me. Always. He's never once laughed at me or told me I was pretending, the way Dad does when something new happens to me. And he doesn't charge me for visits, either. He says if I need him, I can come anytime. Only thing wrong is that sometimes I think Dr. Welty is afraid to tell me how sick I really am.

He came striding over to the table. "Well, Vada," he said. "Let's see how you are."

He didn't even ask what was wrong, and I figured, why give him a hint? He'd see in a minute.

He did all the usual—my ears, eyes, and then my throat.

I could feel the chicken bone swelling up, although now I knew it was a tumor. My larynx.

When he was finished, I said, "So? What is it? Tell me, I can handle it."

He put both hands on my shoulders and smiled at me. "Vada," he said. "You're perfectly healthy."

"Can't be!" I said. "I have all the symptoms. My throat. You can see it, can't you?"

He shook his head no.

"And now here!" I said, pointing to my hair. "My hair, it's falling out."

"Vada," Dr. Welty said quietly, "did they bring Mr. Layton to your house today?"

I looked at my shoes. "Yes."

"Vada, you have to stop this. I know you honestly feel worried. But there's nothing wrong with you. There isn't."

He was trying to protect me. I could *feel* the tumor, had felt it for months. So why didn't he tell me the truth? I'd rather know now than choke to death in the middle of the night. Didn't he know that?

In the waiting room, I motioned to Thomas J

to follow me. We went outside and hopped on our bikes.

"What'd he say is wrong with you?" Thomas J said.

"The whole medical profession is a crock," I said.

If it wasn't, I thought, the doctors would've been able to save my mom.

We rode down some streets, not talking much. Thomas J is good that way. He knows when to talk and when to be quiet.

We turned onto my favorite street—one with big old houses and big old trees. The trees are so big that their branches meet in the middle of the street. It's like riding down the middle of a leafy green tunnel.

"Look, Thomas J," I said after a while. "No hands."

"Oh, yeah?" he said. He took his feet off the pedals and stuck them out to both sides. "Look at this—no feet."

"Wow!" I said. "A real Evel Knievel."

Thomas J is such a dork sometimes. Even though he's eleven like me, he looks about eight because he's so skinny and little. And with his huge glasses magnifying his eyes, he looks like a perfect owl. He's also allergic to everything, which is one reason everybody teases him. He wore a wool sweater to school once, and his face blew up like a balloon. In the cafeteria he has to have a special menu with no eggs or milk, and nothing with tomatoes or even ketchup on it. He can't even eat pizza! And he collects strange things, like cicada shells and butterflies and dead bugs and hornet nests. But he's my best friend. We talk about everything, and we climb trees and fish together, and we even play pretend. I wouldn't let anyone else in the whole world know that I still played pretend.

I do wonder sometimes, though, why he doesn't get more upset when I boss him around. I wouldn't let anyone boss *me* like that. Except that maybe he likes to be bossed. Maybe he's used to it.

We were halfway down the street when suddenly I stopped short.

"Hey, look!" I said, pointing. It was Mr. Bixler, our fifth grade teacher, up on a ladder on the porch of one of the old houses, painting a window. Mr. Bixler! He's the best teacher I've ever had. He's young and not married and really good-looking. If I were going to live, I think I'd like to marry Mr. Bixler. It's maybe dumb, but I imagine sometimes that he'd wait for me, that he'd like to marry me, too—after I grow up, that is.

"Let's go talk to him!" I said to Thomas J.

"I don't want to talk to a teacher!" Thomas J said. "It's summer."

I ignored him.

"Hi, Mr. Bixler!" I called out.

Mr. Bixler looked down and smiled. "Mademoiselle Sultenfuss! And the amazing Dr. J. How's the summer treating you?"

He came off his ladder and over to us, still holding a paintbrush.

"Mr. Bixler, I finished all the books for summer reading."

"All? Already? Summer's just begun."

"I know. But I did. And now I'm reading *War and Peace.*"

"You're not!"

"I am."

"Wow." He smiled. "No wonder you're my prize pupil. And what about you, Dr. J?"

He'd called me his 'prize pupil'! Maybe he *would* wait for me.

"I haven't started on the reading yet," Thomas J said.

"You'd better get on his case, Vada," Mr. Bixler said.

"Mr. Bixler, how come you're painting this house? I didn't know you've always lived here."

"I don't. Well, I didn't, but I do now. I just bought it, and I'm fixing it up."

"It's a big house for one person," I said.

He smiled. "Well, you never can tell."

"Oh," I said.

And I felt devastated. He was getting married!

He *wasn't* going to wait for me.

"Maybe I'll get a pet," he said.

I looked at my hand and twisted my mood ring around for a while, so he wouldn't see how relieved I was. "So where do teachers get money in the summer?" I asked. "I mean, how are you getting money for this house if you're not working?"

He laughed. "I'm teaching a creative writing class at

the community college this summer, starting next week. So I'm doing some work."

"You are? How much does it cost?" I asked.

"The house?"

"No, the class."

"Thirty-five dollars."

"What does a person get for that?"

"Me. For two hours a week. Talking about poetry."

Him. I stared at him. "When is it?" I asked.

"The class? Thursday afternoons, two o'clock." He laughed again. "This is an interrogation, Vada."

"Yeah, well. Guess I'll go home and finish off *War and Peace.*"

"It's summer!" he said, waving the paintbrush at us. "You're kids. Play!"

He turned back to the porch and his ladder, and Thomas J and I got on our bikes.

"Want to go play?" Thomas J said. "How about fishing? Or you want to go to Gray's Orchard and pick some peaches? Or we could try and find cicada shells. I bet they've shed by now."

"Nah," I said—because I had an idea, something I had to do right away. If I could just talk Dad into it.

"I'm going home," I said.

"Home?" Thomas J said. He frowned at me. "How come? It's not dinnertime yet."

"Dinnertime?" I said. "You're just like a dog. You just go home to eat!"

He shrugged.

I headed for home, but he just sat there on his bike.

When I turned, I saw him looking after me, puzzled-looking, pushing at his glasses with his middle finger —like he really couldn't figure out why anyone would go home if it wasn't time to eat.

"Bye, Thomas J!" I called. "Don't pee on the hydrant!"

*M*ean. I was mean to Thomas J. But he shouldn't be so easy to tease. Anyway, he wouldn't stay mad long, if he was even mad at all. And I did have to get home in a hurry. I had a great idea. *If* I could just get Dad to agree—if I could get him to give me the money.

Two hours a week with Mr. Bixler, talking about poetry. Maybe I could even write a poem for Mr. Bixler, tell him I was dying. It could be very romantic. Besides, I've always loved to write. I even write stories and poems when I don't have to.

But it would be hard to get Dad to part with that much money, especially now after he'd just upped what he had to pay Shelly.

But it was worth asking for, if I could just get him in the right mood at the right time. I'd just have to figure out the best time. And maybe the right time would be now, if Shelly was working out good.

At home I dropped my bike on the grass and went in the house looking for Dad.

No Dad in the front of the house or in his office. Not in the back, either. But Gramoo was in the kitchen, rocking in her chair. And something was cooking on the stove, something Dad had probably started earlier. He's been doing all the cooking since Gramoo got weird and stopped doing it. He worries that he's not a good cook.

Actually he's not. But I'd never tell him that because it would hurt his feelings.

"Hi, Gramoo," I said, even though I knew she wouldn't answer. "Where's Dad?"

I heard sounds coming from the basement room, and I went and tugged on the door to open it. When it finally let loose, it almost smacked me in the face.

I could hear voices down there—Dad and Shelly and Uncle Phil.

As I listened, I heard Uncle Phil invite Shelly to meet him at the bar. Uncle Phil is always inviting ladies to meet him at the bar.

I went down a few steps and peeked.

Dad and Uncle Phil and Shelly were all collected around Mr. Layton.

"Dad?" I said softly.

"Bookends," Uncle Phil said, looking down at Mr. Layton. "Walnut bookends."

"I made a tie rack," Dad said.

What were they doing—showing off for Shelly? They had already had this conversation. Uncle Phil is a womanizer—at least, that's what Dad always says.

"Laminated bookends," Uncle Phil said. "I got an A."

"You never got an A in your life," Dad said. He turned to Shelly. "Why don't you give Mr. Layton that haircut?"

I didn't want to watch this!

I scooted back up the stairs. But I was dying of curiosity, too, wondering how Shelly would handle a dead person.

I bet Dad was wondering, too.

So at the top of the stairs, even though I couldn't see anything, I crouched to listen.

"So, Mr. Layton!" I heard Shelly say, like she was talking to a real person—well, I mean to a real live person. "How do you want it cut—wet or dry?"

I fled upstairs to my room.

Later. At dinner I'd ask for the money, if Dad seemed happy.

But at dinner I didn't get a chance to ask. First, the stew was awful, and even though neither of us would tell Dad that, Uncle Phil said he wasn't going to eat much because it would make him fat. And Dad said Uncle Phil was already fat, and even though Dad laughed when he said it, you could tell that it made Uncle Phil feel bad. And then I could see that Dad felt bad.

Dad turned away and picked up a spoon and fed Gramoo little spoonfuls of stew till she seemed to catch on and began doing it herself, the way we always have to do. But Dad's face was red, like he was embarrassed for what he'd said.

Then after a minute, after Gramoo began feeding herself, Dad and Uncle Phil began talking about an accident on I-34 and how they were bringing in two bodies next day.

Bodies! Dead people from an accident. I wondered whose fault that was, that accident. Did the person who caused it feel bad—bad, like I felt about my mom?

Then, to make it worse, Gramoo suddenly began singing those songs she belts out for no reason to no one in particular. This time it was "Anything Goes."

At the top of her lungs she sang while Dad and Uncle Phil talked about accidents and bodies.

And my throat was already hurting like anything.

I couldn't help it. I had to tell them, say something.

"Dad?" I said. I had to practically yell to be heard over Gramoo. "Dad?"

Dad frowned at me. "What?" he said, and he cupped his ear.

"Dad, my throat!" I yelled. "Remember what I told you this morning? It's really bad. It's gotten much worse."

Dad just shook his head and turned back to Uncle Phil.

"I just hate the accident ones," he said. "You can never satisfy the families."

"Tell me about it," Uncle Phil said.

Gramoo kept right on singing.

I took a bite of stew, and suddenly I choked. I mean, really choked. I took a quick sip of water, but I kept right on coughing.

I coughed and spit, and tears came to my eyes. But nobody got up to pat my back or anything.

I left the table and collapsed coughing on the couch across the room just as Shelly came up from the basement.

"Well, I did his hair," she said brightly. "He looks kind of like Danny Kaye if he were Swedish. . . ."

And then she heard me choking, and she rushed to my side. "Sweetie! You all right?" she said, patting me on the back.

I shook my head no.

She patted me some more, hard. I think she was making it worse, but at least she was trying.

She turned to Dad. "Harry!" she said. "She's hurt."

Dad kept right on eating. "She's just pretending," he said. "Vada, come and eat your broccoli."

Pretending?

"I'll get you water," Shelly said. "Stay right there."

"It's my throat," I whispered.

"I know," she said. "I know. I'll get you water."

In a minute she was back with water, and she sat next to me on the couch while I drank it down.

It really did help some.

After a minute Shelly asked, "Want more dinner now?"

I shook my head no.

"Want me to turn on the TV for you?"

I nodded.

She went over and turned on the TV and then went back downstairs. But I saw her squint up her eyes at Dad as she went, like she was thinking about something, maybe like she was mad.

After a minute of watching TV, I suddenly saw something—something great! A rerun of one of Dad's favorite shows was on!

That would put him in a good mood!

"Dad!" I said. "Look! Look at this, your favorite show!"

Dad looked up from the table, then stood up. He came to his regular TV-watching chair, bringing his plate and his glass of club soda with him.

"Hey, Phil," Dad said. "Come watch this. It's so great."

Uncle Phil didn't move, though. He just sat there with Gramoo.

After Dad had settled down, I went over and sat on the floor by his chair.

Dad laughed a few times at what was happening on the TV, and I laughed with him.

Then, when I thought Dad was happy enough, I decided the time was right.

"Dad?" I said. I said it very softly.

"Hush, Vada," Dad said, and he nodded at the TV.

I waited a minute, and then after he had laughed a bunch more times, I tried again. "Dad?" I said, still quietly, looking up at him. "Can I have thirty-five dollars?"

No sense beating around the bush.

"That's a lot of money for a little girl," Dad said, looking down and smiling at me.

"It's for school," I said. "A summer writing class."

Dad pointed to his glass. "Any soda left?" he asked. His eyes were glued to the TV again.

32

I got up and got the soda from the table, poured the rest into his glass, and then sat down on the floor next to him again.

"My teacher said I was a very good writer," I said. "And you know how important it is to get started early on your career, like you did with being an undertaker. You started as a kid, right?"

"I don't know, babe," Dad said. He reached down, sort of absentminded like and patted my head. He kept his hand there for a while, patting my hair softly, like I was a pet dog like Thomas J or something.

But it felt good all the same.

"Turn up the volume, will you?" Dad said then.

Again I got up. I turned up the TV, then came back again to sit beside Dad.

"Daddy?" I said.

He sipped at his soda and laughed out loud at the TV. "Watch this!" he said, waving his glass toward the TV. "I love this guy."

"Dad?" I said again.

"What?"

"The money. Could I have the money?"

For a long minute Dad didn't answer. "Maybe next summer," he said after a while, and he smoothed my hair again. "Umm," he said softly. "Your hair feels nice."

"But, Dad!" I took a deep breath. "How about this—when you go to bingo, I could go, too? Maybe I could *win* the money?"

"No, you can't go to bingo," Dad said. He laughed at the TV again. "That's my one night out alone. You know that."

"Then will you *lend* me the money?" I asked. "I could pay you back."

Dad sighed. "Vada," he said, "you forget certain things. You forget, but I remember." He put his hand under my chin and turned my face up to him. "Last month it was violin," he said. "The time before, it was ventriloquism. Another time, juggling. If you're still interested in writing next summer, then maybe. Okay? But not now."

He let go of my chin and fixed all his attention on the TV again.

I sighed and got up.

Slowly I went upstairs.

Ha!

He forgot about the time I wanted to be a magician. I was really great at making myself disappear.

CHAPTER

V

*B*efore I went to sleep, I went to my closet and pulled out my old record player—the only one I have to play the old, old records on. I put on a favorite old record—"Wedding Bell Blues." Then I went to my desk and got out my class picture—the one that has Mr. Bixler right smack in the middle. I'm next to him. I arranged it that way on picture-taking day.

"Somehow," I whispered to him. "Somehow I'll come up with a plan. I'll do it. You just wait and see."

And by the next morning I did have a plan, a wonderful one, a way to get the money I needed. I got up super early and went over to Thomas J's, taking my fishing pole with me. I had called Thomas J the night before and told him to be ready to go fishing, but I didn't tell him my plan yet.

When I got to his house, Thomas J was all ready, except first he said he had to go pee.

"Want to play our game?" I said, as he headed for the bathroom.

"Sure," he said, grinning.

I knew what that meant—he really had to go. Bad.

"I'll count," I said.

Thomas J went in and shut the door.

Through the closed door, he shouted, "Okay, start! And no fair counting slow. Not a thousand and one, that way."

"Okay, okay," I said.

I heard him begin peeing, and I started counting, regular, not too slow. "One, two, three, four . . .

"Hey! Too slow!" he yelled.

"Five!" I said, fast and loud. "Six, seven—"

He was finished.

"Seven," I said.

"Eight!" he shouted back.

But he'd finished peeing before the eight.

"Seven," I said back. "I counted seven."

"Seven and a half," he said.

He came out of the bathroom, still fixing his pants.

"Okay," I said, "Seven and a half. But bet I can do it longer."

"Bet," he said. "Not even six."

"My turn," I said.

I went in the bathroom and closed and locked the door. Then, very quietly, I went to the sink, got the water glass, and turned on the faucet. Slowly, quietly, I let the glass fill up with water.

"Hey! Hurry up in there!" Thomas J yelled.

"Hold your horses," I said. "It takes girls longer."

When the glass was full, I went to the toilet.

"Okay!" I yelled. "And not too slow. Start!"

Then slowly I began pouring the water into the bowl.

I could hear Thomas J counting. "One, two, three, four . . ."

He was deliberately going slow.

"Count!" I yelled.

"Five, six, seven," he said. Slow. And sulky. "Eight."

"I win!" I yelled.

I flushed the toilet, then waited long enough so he would think I was getting myself fixed and all, and then came out. "I win!" I said. "I can pee longer than you."

Together we went out on the porch to get our fishing poles.

"You always win," Thomas J said, even though it wasn't true.

"That's because my mom was an Arabian princess. They can hold their water like a camel."

"She was not!" Thomas J said.

I jumped on him suddenly and wrestled him to the porch floor. His glasses flew off.

I sat on him. Hard. "Say my mother was an Arabian princess," I said.

"No!" he yelled.

I bounced up and down on his back.

"Ouch!" he yelled.

"Say it!" I said.

I bounced again.

"Okay, okay," he said. "She was an Arabian princess."

I bounced again. "And the most beautiful woman in the whole world," I said.

"And the most beautiful woman. Get off!" he said. I did.

We both sat up, catching our breath.

Thomas J found his glasses and put them back on.

I bet my mother *was* beautiful. Funny, not to ever know. I'd seen pictures, but . . . I wondered if she stayed mad at me, like in heaven if she was mad.

Suddenly Thomas J jumped up, grabbed his pole, and raced down the steps. "Your mother looked like the Mona Lisa!" he shouted.

I raced after him. "Don't you say that about my mother!"

He ran down the sidewalk toward the lake.

I don't know why he bothers running. He must know I can always catch him.

I grabbed my pole and caught up to him in less than a block, just at the edge of the lake.

Thomas J circled away from me, keeping the willow tree between him and me.

But I wasn't interested in catching him anymore. I was more interested in my plan for making money.

"Hey, Thomas J," I said. "What about this—what if we catch some fish? Catch them and sell them. We can advertise fresh fish and say how people don't have to go to market or anything. We'll bring them to them fresh from the bay."

"Bay?" Thomas J said, looking out over the small lake.

"Well, you know. What do you think?"

He shrugged. "I don't know. Will anyone really buy sunnies?"

"If we catch big ones they might. And anyway, maybe there are other fish in the lake. Maybe there's . . . I don't know, trout or something."

"Yeah!" Thomas J said. "Maybe salmon, even."

I didn't know about that. Didn't salmon come from big streams or something—really *big* ones in the North?

Anyway, it didn't matter. What mattered was getting money.

"What do you need money for?" he asked.

"That writing class," I said.

"You're going to *school* in the *summer?*" Thomas J said. "Is it because of Mr. Bixler?"

I wasn't going to answer that.

"It's not exactly school," I said. "Come on, bait the hooks."

Together, we put the lures on the hooks and dropped the hooks into the water.

We sat there with our poles for a long time. But our lines were as still as if all the fish were dead.

"Nothing's biting," I said.

"Maybe they all had a big breakfast," Thomas J said. "I could lend you some money. I have five dollars in my piggy bank."

"Thanks," I said. "But I'd still need another thirty. We'll catch something eventually. Let's hook our lines here over the branch. Then we can get up in the tree."

So we dropped the lines over one of the low-hanging willow branches and let them dangle in the water that way.

Then Thomas J and I both climbed up in the tree.

Thomas J hooked his legs over a branch and swung upside down, letting his arms dangle over his head. As he flipped himself over, his glasses fell off.

"Look at me," he said. "I'm going to be an acrobat when I grow up."

"Big deal," I said. "I can do that. And my glasses won't fall off, either."

"That's because you don't wear any."

"Duh."

Thomas J straightened up then. "Can you be an acrobat if you're scared of being up in high places?" he asked.

I shrugged. "Why not? You'll get over it. I bet my dad was scared of dead people when he first started. He got over it. Hey, look!"

"What?"

"You got something. Your bobber! It's jiggling!"

It was dancing around like he had a *big* fish.

I jumped off the branch, and Thomas J jumped down, too. But he fell as he jumped, and landed on both knees.

He is *so* clumsy! He was pawing around on the ground, looking for his glasses while I ran to the water.

"I can't find them!" Thomas J yelled from behind me. "I can't see. Where are they?"

"I'll help you in a minute!" I said. "I gotta reel him in."

I grabbed his pole and began reeling the fish in.

But in a minute Thomas J was beside me, glasses on. He grabbed the rod out of my hand and reeled it in the rest of the way. On the hook was a sunny—a *very* small sunny, not even as big as my hand.

"It's only a sunny," I said. "No one will buy that. Throw it back."

"I don't like touching fish," Thomas J said. He looked at me.

I don't like touching fish, either. He knew that. So I wasn't offering.

When Thomas J saw that I wasn't offering, he looked around. "I know what," he said.

He laid the fish on the ground, then lightly put his foot on it. "I'm going to pull the hook out without having to touch him," he said. "Watch this."

He pulled on the line. I could see the hook yanking at the fish's mouth.

"You're hurting him!" I said. "Don't kill him."

"I'm not trying to," Thomas J said. He pulled again, more gently. But I could see that the fish's mouth was still getting pulled sideways.

I pushed Thomas J out of the way and picked up the fish. Very gently, I wriggled the hook until it was loose.

It took a long time, but I didn't twist the fish's mouth anymore.

When it was finally out, I threw the fish back in the water. But as I did, the line snapped back suddenly, and the hook snagged my thumb.

"Ouch!" I yelled. "My thumb!"

"What?" Thomas J said. He came over to me, trying to look over my shoulder, but I turned away, my thumb in my mouth.

I didn't want him to see that I was almost crying.

"You okay?" Thomas J asked.

"Yeah. How about the fish? Is the fish all right?" I asked, my back turned to him.

Thomas J didn't answer for a minute.

I turned around, still sucking my thumb.

Thomas J was standing at the edge of the lake looking in the water.

"Did he swim away?" I asked.

"Yeah, he's all right," Thomas J said.

But when he turned to me, his face was beet red.

He was lying, I knew. He always turns red when he lies.

Poor fish! I had killed him.

"Let me see!" I said, and I started toward the edge of the lake.

But Thomas J said, "Let's go!" And he started pushing me back. "I'm tired of fishing. Let me see your thumb."

I let him see.

"It's bleeding," he said.

"Yeah."

And then I had an idea—something I had read about lots of times. And since I didn't have a real brother or sister, or a mother . . .

"Want to be blood brothers?" I said, holding up my bleeding thumb.

"No, I don't want to. Come on."

"All you'd have to do is pick that scab on your arm."

"It's a mosquito bite."

"It'll bleed," I said.

He sighed. He was still standing between me and the place where I had tossed the fish back.

"If I do it, can we go?" he said.

"Yes."

Thomas J sat down and began picking at the scab on his arm. He didn't even make a face like it was hurting or anything, although it must have hurt a little. It was just like he was a little kid in school, doing something he'd been told to do.

I felt a little bad about it then, hoping it didn't hurt him, really.

When it finally began to bleed, he held out his arm.

"Okay," he said. "Here."

"Hold still," I said. And I rubbed my finger on the bleeding place.

"There," I said. "Now we're blood brothers for life."

"Okay," Thomas J muttered, but he didn't sound particularly thrilled.

We stood up and picked up our fishing poles and started for home.

"Does it feel different?" I asked, when we were halfway down the block.

"What? The scab?"

I poked him. "No, dummy. Being blood brothers?"

He didn't answer for a minute. And then he said, "Does it to you?"

"I asked you first," I said.

He didn't look at me. "No," he said finally.

We were quiet for a while.

"Does it to you?" he asked.

"No," I answered, because I'm almost always honest with Thomas J.

"It doesn't matter," Thomas J said softly. "We're practically brothers, anyway."

Thomas J and I got back to my house just as Shelly was coming out onto the porch. She plopped down on the steps, kind of mad-looking.

I sat down on the step beside her, and Thomas J sat on her other side. There was a basketball there, and I picked it up and began bouncing it between my feet.

"What's the matter?" I said to Shelly. "You mad or something?"

"Not mad. But your dad didn't like what I did with Reverend Porter's wife." She sighed. "Mrs. Porter looked like an old schoolmarm, so I highlighted her cheekbones with blush. And her lips, they were too thin, so I made them . . . sensual!"

"So what's the matter with that?" I asked.

Shelly sighed again. "Your father said that Mrs. Porter never had sensual lips in her life, so I had to do her over. Then he told me to mind my own business about you. . . ."

"Me? What about me?"

But she just shrugged and pulled a candy bar out of her purse and began unwrapping it.

"Look!" Thomas J said, pointing.

It was Megan and Lisa coming down the street arm in arm, with Judy trailing along behind.

Megan and Lisa are the prettiest girls in class—and the meanest. Judy's nice, though. The problem is, Judy's new and she doesn't know better than to hang around with Megan and Lisa. She'd better learn, though, or she'll end up just like them.

They stopped near the curb by Shelly's camper.

"Look, it's Vada and her little boyfriend," Megan said, just loud enough to make sure I heard. "Aren't they sweet, playing basketball together?"

"He's not my boyfriend," I yelled. "And we're not playing basketball. I'm *holding* the ball. Can't you tell the difference?"

"I bet she kisses him on the lips!" Lisa said.

Megan laughed hysterically, like Lisa had said the funniest thing ever.

I pointed at Thomas J. "Do you think I'd kiss that ugly thing?" I said.

"Yeah, anyway!" Thomas J said.

I just gave Thomas J a *look*. Dummy! Didn't he know he was insulting himself?

Suddenly he made a face back at me, like he had just figured it out.

"Let's leave the lovers," Megan said. "We have something better to do anyway."

"Yeah," Lisa said. "Judy's father owns the new movies, and we get to see all the movies we want—for free!"

"You want to come sometime?" Judy said, smiling up at me. And she smiled at Thomas J, too. "You can if you want. My dad would let you."

"Ew!" Marcia said. "Don't invite her. She'll have to bring her *boyfriend*. And he might bring all his little dead moths or something."

Megan slid her arm through Lisa's again, and then the two of them started down the street. For just a minute Judy stood looking at us; then she hurried after them.

When they were halfway down the block, I could hear Megan and Lisa chanting this stupid baby song: "Vada and Thomas J sitting in a tree, k-i-s-s-i-n-g. First comes love. Then comes marriage. Then comes TJ in a baby carriage."

I made a face at their backs. They could at least come up with something original, something that didn't sound like they were in second grade. But it was always the same, had been for years. They were jealous of me and Thomas J being friends, that's all.

"Want some chocolate?" Shelly said, holding the candy bar out toward me.

I shook my head no. Those snobs. Jerks.

"Chocolate?" Shelly said to Thomas J.

"Can't," he said. "I'm allergic to it."

"To *chocolate?*" Shelly said.

"He's allergic to everything," I said irritably.

"Vada," Shelly said, "you shouldn't let those girls upset you."

I thumped the basketball hard. "I'm not *upset,*" I said. "I'd never hang out with those snobs, anyway. I only surround myself with people who are . . ."

What? What was Thomas J?

I didn't know. Except he was my friend. My blood brother. Then why was I suddenly so irritated with him?

None of us said anything for a while.

"Pretty ring you're wearing," Shelly said, looking down at my hand.

"It's a mood ring," I said. "It tells what mood I'm in."

I looked down at it, too. Uncle Phil brought it back for me when he went to Miami last year. It's supposed to turn colors, from blue to green and gray and black, depending on your mood.

It stays black on me practically all the time. Like now.

"It doesn't work," Thomas J said. "It always stays black."

"It's only black when you're around," I said. "You put me in a bad mood."

"Maybe black means you're happy?" Shelly said.

I shrugged. "I don't think so. Shelly, how can I get thirty-five dollars?"

"What do you need it for?" Shelly asked.

"She's crazy," Thomas J said. "She wants to go to school over the summer."

I made a face at him. "It's not real school, it's a writing class. I want to be a writer."

Thomas J grinned. "She only wants to take it 'cause her sweetie pie's the teacher."

"Shush up!" I said, and I pushed him, but not really hard.

"Well, I think you'd be a fine writer," Shelly said. "Maybe someday you'll even write a book like Jacqueline Susann. Did you ask your dad?"

"He won't give it to me," I said.

"I gotta go," Thomas J said. "It's lunchtime. I told my mom I'd be home for lunch."

I got up and began dribbling the basketball across the porch.

"So go," I said.

I didn't say, "Don't pee on the hydrant," like I did yesterday. But I thought it just the same.

And I hoped the snobby girls turned and looked. They'd see Thomas J and I don't spend *all* our time together.

I dribbled the ball across the porch the way Uncle Phil said I should, trying not to look at it. I was getting better at it, but it was hard. I wondered if I should try to be a basketball player when I grew up. Maybe I'd be the first girl in the professional leagues. I was learning a lot this summer, mostly from Uncle Phil. He's really good. He says that once he was almost in the pros. And Daddy likes basketball. He watches it all the time on TV.

I practiced some more, trying to dribble without looking at the ball. I was actually getting pretty good.

Maybe I'd show Dad. He'd be impressed.

I opened the front door.

"You coming, Shelly?" I said over my shoulder.

"In a minute," she answered.

I went in the house, still bouncing the ball, still not looking.

"Hey, Dad?" I yelled.

No answer.

I went on through to the back, but no one was there—no Dad, no Uncle Phil, nobody. Just Gramoo, rocking slowly.

The basement door was open.

"Dad?" I called down.

No answer.

"Dad, you down there?"

And then suddenly the ball was gone. It bounced away from me and down the steps.

Down the steps.

"Dad!" I yelled. "Dad, are you down there?"

Still no answer.

Very slowly I went down the stairs—but not all the way. I stopped, like always, on the bottom step.

"Dad?" I called softly.

Dad wasn't there—but somebody was. Well, some *body* was. On the table. Probably that Mrs. Porter that Shelly had been talking about.

Oh, gross.

But I had to get my ball. What to do?

The body wouldn't hurt me. Dead people were . . . dead. Right?

I took a deep breath. I looked around, then stepped off the bottom step.

Then I raced over to the ball, snatched it up, and ran back for the stairs as if the dead were chasing me.

I ran all the way up, clutching the ball. Safe. The body hadn't moved.

50

But when I got to the top, the door was closed! Closed! And I'd left it open. I knew I had.

I turned the handle and pushed.

Nothing.

It was stuck!

I threw myself against it. But it didn't budge. And my ball rolled away again and down the stairs.

"Oh, help!" I yelled. "Let me out. Please, help!"

I looked over my shoulder. From here I couldn't see the body on the table. Had it moved?

I shoved at the door again, but it wouldn't budge.

"Help!" I pounded on the door. "Oh, help, help! She's going to get me. Help!"

I was stuck.

Sing! Sing! Gramoo said to sing. It keeps the scary stuff away.

I rattled the doorknob.

"Help me!" I shouted. "Oh, please. Help."

I began singing and crying at the same time. "Oh, help! Doo wah diddy . . . help!"

I was sobbing. Oh, stupid me. Where was Dad? Gramoo? Uncle Phil? Somebody!

I pounded on the door again. And suddenly it swung open so fast I almost fell out—out and into Shelly's arms.

"Shelly!" I cried.

"Vada!" she said. "What happened?"

"My ball. I lost my ball!" I was sobbing. "It went downstairs and I got locked in!"

I turned and kicked the door.

Shelly put her arms around me. "Come on, sweetheart," she said. "It's okay."

I pulled away. Gramoo. I wanted Gramoo.

I ran to Gramoo and practically jumped into her lap. I buried my head in her chest.

"Gramoo!" I cried.

Why couldn't I stop crying? This was so dumb!

"Vada!" Shelly said, coming to me and crouching beside me. "Vada, it's all right. Don't be frightened. You know what my mother used to do when I got scared?"

I didn't answer. I just hugged Gramoo tighter, still crying.

But Gramoo didn't hug back. She probably didn't even know I was there.

I felt like pummeling her with both fists. Listen to me! I wanted to scream. Try! You know I'm here.

"Listen, Vada," Shelly continued, even though I didn't answer her. "My mother said I should close my eyes and imagine the most beautiful place in the whole world. A place with rainbows and flowers and horses to ride. And she said as long as I was thinking of it, I'd always be safe."

"Gramoo used to say I should sing," I said, my voice still shaky. "She said it would make me not scared. That's what she said."

"Well, that too," Shelly said.

"It didn't work," I said.

"Try my way, then," Shelly said softly.

I couldn't. I was too scared to close my eyes. All I'd see would be that body, that dead body. I just kept hiding in Gramoo's chest, but my eyes were open.

"What were you scared of?" I finally asked.

"Me? Well, when I was your age, my uncle took me to see *The Wizard of Oz*. Did you ever see it?"

I nodded.

"Well, I was afraid of the Munchkins."

I sat up and looked at her. "You mean the flying monkeys."

"No," Shelly said. "The Munchkins. I couldn't sleep at night because I thought they lived under my bed."

"But the Munchkins are good," I said. "Everybody likes them."

"I thought they'd get me," Shelly said. "Come on, Vada." She held out her hands to me. "Let go of Gramoo. You're too big to be sitting on her lap."

I untwisted myself from Gramoo and stood up.

Gramoo began to rock again, slowly, slowly.

I brushed at my jeans. "Were there willow trees in your special place?" I asked.

"Yes," Shelly said. "I think there were willow trees."

"Okay." I nodded. I straightened my shirt and jeans. "I'm all right now," I said. "I'm completely recovered."

CHAPTER

VII

*F*or the rest of that day I hung around in my room, recovering from being scared half to death. And also trying to come up with some method of getting that thirty-five dollars by next Thursday. I knew there was a way, if I could just think one up. I thought of washing dogs and cats, and I thought of walking dogs and cats, and I even thought of baby-sitting babies, even though I don't much like any baby. But even though I thought and thought, nothing came to me, not one single thing that would work in time.

Finally I had an idea. Not a money idea, but maybe a place to get an idea—Uncle Phil. He has lots of money and is always coming up with schemes to get more. Mostly, they involve women—at least, that's what Dad says—but maybe he'd have an idea that would work for me.

That night I went downstairs and to the kitchen. Gramoo was there, but no Uncle Phil.

"Where's Phil?" I asked Gramoo.

She just rocked and rocked.

I went over and stood beside her, my hand on her hair, like I had done the other day.

"How you doing, Gramoo?" I asked.

No answer.

"Gramoo?" I said again, "look at me."

She was bent over, her head down, looking over her knees at her shoes.

What was she thinking about? Was she lonely in there?

Since I couldn't see her face, I got down on my hands and knees. That way I could sort of look up into her face.

For a minute, looking at her from upside down like that, I was almost sure she was looking back at me, knew who I was.

"You okay?" I whispered. "You hear me?"

She blinked.

"You *can* hear me, can't you?" I said.

And then she blinked again, and I thought I saw tears in her eyes.

I touched her face, but her cheek was dry.

"You okay?" I whispered. "Why won't you talk?"

I patted her cheek then, gently, over and over. It was soft, more than soft, like flesh without any bones underneath.

But there was no other sign she had heard me at all. Her eyes seemed just as blank as they'd been for ages.

I stood up, then patted her hair a little again and brought her a drink of water.

She took a few sips, like she does sometimes, like water is one thing she notices and cares about.

After she drank it down, I went out. I closed and locked the door behind me.

We have to do that—lock Gramoo up at night when there's a viewing going on and in the daytime if there's a funeral, to be sure she doesn't just wander in on people. She did that a few times when she first got weird, and scared people half to death.

After I had her locked up, I went to the front, to the casket room, still looking for Uncle Phil.

And there he was, standing in front of an open casket, both hands on the lid, just standing there looking in.

"Uncle Phil?" I said softly.

He spun around.

"Don't scare me like that," he said, a hand on his chest. "You'll give me a heart attack." But he grinned at me.

I smiled back.

Uncle Phil is really very good-looking for an old person. He must be at least as old as Dad. He fought in some war somewhere, and he had a steel plate put in his head. Dad says he's never been the same since. I wouldn't know, because he's always been the same to me. One night Uncle Phil said he picked up a radio station from Oklahoma in his teeth. That must have been really neat.

"Uncle Phil?" I said. "How can I get money?"

"Work," he said. "work hard, like me."

"What kind of work?" I said.

"Do what I do. It's good money."

I shuddered. I was not working with dead people, that was for sure. And I was too young to be a bartender like him.

"I don't mean when I grow up," I said. "I mean now, today."

He waved a hand at me. "Play! Be a kid. Don't worry about work."

This wasn't helping any. He sounded just like Mr. Bixler.

And then I had a sudden idea. "Want to play Scrabble?" I said. "We could play for money. I could go get the game?"

"Not now," Uncle Phil said. "I'm hiding from your dad. He wants me to do some chores. I want to take a nap. Is Gramoo locked up?"

I nodded. And then I said, "Uncle Phil, is she mad at me?"

"Gramoo?" Uncle Phil said. "Mad at you?"

"She doesn't talk to me anymore. Is it my fault she stopped talking to everybody? You know, that she's mad at me or something?"

"Vada, she's old. She's senile."

"How long's she going to stay senile for?"

"Vada, sweetie," Uncle Phil said. "People don't get better from it. You know that. Your dad told you that."

"But not *ever?* He didn't say not ever."

Uncle Phil shook his head. "Not ever."

He was looking into the casket again.

Not ever? Ever?

She'd never rock me and tell me how my mom would have loved me and how she, Gramoo, loved me more than anything?

I didn't believe she'd never get better.

"Uncle Phil," I said. "Remember when Gramoo used to dance with me? I'd stand on her feet and she'd twirl me around and we'd sing and Dad would play his tuba? Remember? That was just a little while ago. You used to dance, too."

"Still do," he said. "Still do!"

He was running his hands over the lining inside the casket, like he was feeling the material, deciding if he wanted to buy it.

It gave me the creeps to watch him do that.

"Why are you a womanizer?" I asked him.

"What?" He turned back to me. "Where did you hear that?"

"Daddy said you are."

"Well, a little of that might do wonders for your dad."

"Of what?"

"You'll find out someday."

"Is he mad at me?"

"Who? Your dad? Why would he be mad at you? What's this all about?"

I just shrugged. I couldn't tell him why I thought Dad was mad at me—not the real reason, anyway.

So all I said was "He doesn't talk to me much, either."

"He's got a lot on his mind," Uncle Phil said. "With Gramoo sick, he's got to do so much now—laundry and cooking and his job and all. Now look, I've got one of my headaches, so be a good girl and let me sleep for a while, okay?" He took off his shoes, laid them gently inside the casket, then put one foot over the side, preparing to climb in.

"You're sleeping in there?" I said.

"One of the quietest places in this world," he said, grinning.

As I watched, he settled into the casket, sliding down, smiling as he nestled his head onto the pink satin pillow.

I shuddered, but I just said, "Okay. 'Night."

"Nighty-night," he said, smiling.

I went out and shut the door behind me. As I turned, I saw him pull the lid halfway down over himself.

How could he *sleep* in a casket? Wouldn't he be afraid he'd never wake up? He is *too* weird.

I know I would—be afraid of never waking up, that is.

I went back upstairs, thinking. Uncle Phil was nice, but he was wrong. It was probably just what Dad had said—he hadn't been the same since they put that plate in his head. He didn't understand things. Because it couldn't be that Gramoo would never talk to me again. He was just saying that because he didn't know when she *would* begin.

I went upstairs to my room and sat on my bed. Another whole day with Gramoo not speaking. Another whole day and I was no closer than before to getting that money—the money I needed to be with Mr. Bixler.

CHAPTER

VIII

*N*ext morning I was out on the porch jumping rope with Thomas J, still thinking about the money. I had no idea where to get it, and class was starting in just two days.

I had one end of the rope tied to the porch swing, and I was turning the other end.

Thomas J was jumping, at the same time telling me about this great giant slug he had found that morning.

"It was as big as my hand!" he said, panting.

"Yuck!" I said. "How can you stand crawly things like that?"

"They don't crawl," Thomas J said. He was breathing really hard, a little whistling noise coming out with each breath. "They slither."

Thomas J isn't supposed to jump rope. It's bad for his asthma, but he does it anyway.

"Gross!" I said.

"Not gross. They're nice," Thomas J wheezed. "I'm up to sixty!"

I wanted him to stop, but I didn't dare tell him. He gets really mad if he thinks I'm trying to take care of him.

I think one reason we're friends is that I don't act like he's a frail little baby, like everybody else does.

But I couldn't let him wheeze like that.

"Hey!" I said. "There's Shelly."

She had just pulled up in her camper.

"Let's ask her if we can look around inside her camper. Want to?"

"No. I want to jump."

But his face was deep red, almost purple.

"Come on," I said. "Let's do it." I dropped my end of the rope.

Thomas J tripped. "Hey!" he yelled. "What'd you do that for?"

"I didn't *do* anything," I said. "Come on."

Thomas J got up, pushed his glasses firmly back on his nose, and followed me to the camper.

We waited on the curb while Shelly parked it.

As she opened the door to get out, I said, "Can we look around inside your camper?"

She looked at her watch. "Sure," she said. "I have time. Come on in. I'll give you the royal tour."

Thomas J went up the steps first, and I followed him. I could still hear the little whistles in his breath, but not as loud.

Shelly followed me in.

There were ropes made of brown and green beads hanging between the driver's part and the back part. Thomas J pushed them aside and we went in.

Wow! Neat. There was a tiny couch, kind of cream-colored, and a white wooden table with a matching bench and some wall cabinets and a stove and a tiny refrigerator. There was a little red and white striped rug on the floor, and white curtains with daisies on them on the windows. There was a cookie jar shaped like a dog on the table, and one red plastic rose in a vase on a plastic lace doily. On the wall over the table was a little brown wooden cuckoo clock and a shelf of books. There were even tiny towels on the tiny sink.

I loved it! It was just like a regular house, only very little and on wheels.

"Where's your bed?" I asked.

Shelly pointed to the couch that ran along one side near the back.

"It folds up," she said.

"Wow, cool!" I said. "Really cool. I wish I had one like this."

"Can you really eat and sleep here?" Thomas J said.

"Yep," Shelly answered. "Can and do."

Thomas J jumped behind the steering wheel then, clutching it tightly, making noises like he was pretending to be driving. "I'm driving us to Liverpool," he said.

"Liverpool?" Shelly asked.

"Yeah," I said softly. "He's a big Ringo fan."

"Oh," Shelly said. "Would you guys like something? A soda?"

"I would!" I said.

Thomas J was still making driving noises and hadn't heard her.

"Thomas J?" Shelly repeated, louder. "A soda?"

"Yes, please," Thomas J said.

Shelly opened the tiny refrigerator and took out two sodas and put them on the table.

Thomas J stopped driving and came and sat across from me. He wasn't so red, and—at least from across the table—I couldn't hear his breath whistling anymore.

"Isn't this great?" he said. "Don't you wish you had one?"

I nodded. I did. I'd love to drive away somewhere in this.

Shelly got out some ice cube trays and shook out the cubes.

"Hey!" Thomas J said, poking at his glasses. "Look at how small those ice cubes are."

But I was looking at a book I'd taken off the shelf. It was a love story, with a picture of a man and a woman on the cover, looking deep into each other's eyes.

Wow. The guy was good-looking, too, even better-looking than Uncle Phil. And the way he was looking at the woman . . . I didn't think anyone would ever look at me like that. Not that I wanted them to or anything.

Shelly came back with the ice in some glasses, poured the sodas, and then gave them to us. "I don't think you should be looking at that," she said to me, nodding at the book. "It's a little too old for you."

I put it down, shrugging, and picked up my soda.

Too old? What'd she think I was—a baby?

Shelly put the book on the shelf with the other books. I could see that they were all the same kind of story—all romance novels, all the same pink cover with a man and a woman looking at each other.

"Did you read all those books?" I asked.

She nodded.

"What are they about? Romance and stuff?"

"Not 'stuff,'" she said, laughing. And then she said, "Love." She said it soft, dreamy-like.

"Oh, gross," Thomas J said.

"Oh, I don't know," Shelly said. "They're just fun to read."

"Are you married?" I asked her.

"No, I'm divorced."

"Daddy says it's bad when people get divorced," I said.

Shelly sighed. "It is. But sometimes married people find out they just can't live together."

"Megan's parents are divorced," Thomas J said.

Shelly turned away and started patting the books into a neat row.

Thomas J reached over then and lifted the lid of the cookie jar—the dog's head part. "Is it all right if I have a cookie?" he asked. And then he said, "Hey, where are the cookies?"

Because when he brought his hand out, instead of cookies, he had a handful of dollar bills.

Shelly turned around. "Oops!" She made a face. "You found my special hiding place. My savings."

"What are you saving for?" Thomas J said, dropping the money back in.

"Nothing special," Shelly said. "Just putting it away for a rainy day."

Why do grown-ups say such dumb things? What's a "rainy day," anyway?

Suddenly, right over Thomas J's head, a cuckoo bird jumped out of the clock. It shouted "Cuckoo!" once, then disappeared back inside its little house.

It scared the wits out of me. And out of Thomas J, too.

He jumped up and poked at his glasses. "Uh-oh," he said. "I was supposed to be home for lunch. Thanks, Shelly. See you, Vada."

And he left, tripping on the little rug on his way out.

Shelly stood up, straightened the rug with her foot, then took Thomas J's glass to the sink. "Well, Miss Vada," she said. "What do you say we go back over?"

I stood up slowly. Very slowly. An idea was forming—a terrible idea. "Can I use your bathroom first?" I said.

Shelly laughed. "Everyone wants to use the tiny bathroom."

"Yeah," I said. I laughed, too. And hoped it sounded real. My mouth felt frozen stiff.

"Well," I said. "But listen, you don't have to wait. Daddy'll be mad if you're late, anyway."

She looked at her watch. "You're right," she said. "Just slam the door when you come out, okay?"

"Okay," I said.

She pushed aside the beads at the front and went out.

After she left, I watched her from the window. She

walked funny, sort of wiggling as she went, her rear end swaying.

As soon as I saw her go up the walk and inside the house, I turned and went back to the table.

My heart was pounding like mad. But nobody would ever know. And I *would* pay her back. Somehow. I'd work or I'd baby-sit. And I'd give up all my allowance till the end of summer. So it wasn't really stealing.

But I'd never stolen anything—taken anything—in my life. Well, that's not true—I did, once. I remember once in the supermarket, I ate a whole bag of M&M's while Gramoo was talking to Mrs. Sennet. And then I stuffed the empty bag behind the bread. But I was only five when I did that. Now . . .

I put a hand on my throat. My throat was suddenly so dried up. And the lump . . . I swallowed hard.

But I *would* give the money back.

Then I reached in the jar and took out a handful of bills.

I counted them quickly, not wanting to take any more than I needed.

I got thirty-five dollars—three tens, five ones— then stuffed the rest back in the jar. The jar still felt heavy and looked pretty full. But I fluffed the rest of the money up so it looked even more full.

She'd never know. And it really wasn't stealing, not if I was going to give it back.

For some reason then something came to my head—a clear picture of something that happened in second grade. My class went swimming at the Y, and I found a hair ball in one of the showers and I don't know why, but I ate it. But I do know that it tasted better than the castor oil that Mrs. Baublitz made me drink afterward.

Weird, to remember that just now. But nobody would make me drink castor oil, or do anything like that. This wasn't anything bad like eating hair balls. This was just borrowing money.

Borrowing it.

CHAPTER

IX

On Thursday I waited till right before it was time for the class to start. Then I raced to the community college and signed up and paid for the course—thirty-five dollars. For a terrible minute I thought the lady at the desk was going to ask where I got so much money. Like Daddy had said, it was a lot of money for a kid.

But she hardly even looked at me. All she said was "Room one forty-two. Around the corner on your right."

And she gave me a little card that said I was allowed to go to class, and a name tag.

I wrote my name on the tag and stuck it on my shirt. Then I went down the hall and around the corner to room 142.

It was a big room with lots of windows and a door that led outside to a courtyard with trees.

There were a lot of people standing around just inside the door. Mr. Bixler was at the desk in front, doing something with some papers. He didn't see me come in.

He wasn't wearing his regular school clothes, a tie and jacket, like he wears in our school. Instead, he was wearing jeans and a T-shirt, sort of like what he was wearing painting the other day. I wondered if there were different rules for grown-up school and kids' school.

I also wondered if he'd gotten his pet.

I went in and slid into a seat. Mr. Bixler still hadn't noticed me.

I looked at the men and women there. Some of them were *weird*-looking, and all of them were *old*. There wasn't anyone even near my age. Also, there wasn't any woman who was extra pretty who Mr. Bixler might like, although there was one who was sort of pretty. Her name tag said Ronda, and she had long black hair and was wearing a long skirt and a tight shirt with a belt around the waist, and boots. Boots! In the middle of the summer. She seemed to be with this scuzzy-looking guy named Justin with a beard and some beads around his neck, the kind of beads like girls wear. Wow! Were they Ronda's beads? Anyway, if Ronda was with him, I was pretty sure she wouldn't be after Mr. Bixler.

They were talking to two men—one with a name tag that said Charles and one named Ray.

Charles was super-thin with a pointy nose, pointy chin, and points even on his wrists and elbows. He was wearing real skinny silver-rimmed glasses, not the chunky, beat-up kind like Thomas J wears. He looked like an accountant.

Ray was short and chubby, with a nice face that made him look a little bit like Santa Claus without the beard. But his fingernails and knuckles were dirty. I bet he worked in a garage or something.

At a desk near me there was a lady named Betty—a mother, you could tell that. She looked tired. And next to Betty was Mrs. Hunsacker! Mrs. Hunsacker? She's our town librarian, and she's at least a hundred years old. Why was she taking a course about poetry?

There was a bunch of other people, too, but they were in the back and I couldn't see their name tags from here. I wondered why so many came to take a course in the middle of the summer. I also tried to figure out how much Mr. Bixler got paid for this.

I was so excited to be here—with him, yet not in regular school. I wondered if he'd be happy to see me, his prize pupil.

I even had a poem ready, just in case.

Did the thirty-five dollars go right to him? Or did it go to the college and they paid him?

Either way, it couldn't be a lot of money.

And thinking about the money made me feel nervous again. But I would pay Shelly back.

In a minute Mr. Bixler asked everyone to sit down.

He said it in his usual nice way, just the way he talks to kids in class. That's what's good about him—he talks to kids just like they're grown-ups and to grown-ups like they're kids, everybody all the same.

When everyone was seated and quiet, Mr. Bixler began reading from a paper in his hand.

" 'The great way is not difficult for those who have no preferences,' " he read in this soft, low voice. " 'When love and hate are both absent, everything becomes clear and undisguised.' "

He put the paper down and looked over the class, a very solemn kind of look. "What do you think the poet is trying to tell us here?"

Blank stares from everyone.

Wow! Grown-ups are just like kids in class.

I raised my hand.

And Mr. Bixler almost fell over backwards.

"Vada?" he said. "Vada Sultenfuss? What are you doing here?"

"Taking a writing course," I said. "I paid my money. And the poet means that if you don't care about anybody—no problem. The big problem is only when you *do* care."

He just stared at me.

"I want to be a writer," I said.

"But this is an adult poetry class," he said.

I felt like saying, "Well, I'm an adult poet." But of course I didn't. I didn't want him to throw me out. Could he do that—if this was just for grown-up poets?

"Hey!" Justin said, jiggling his beads like he wanted to be sure everyone noticed them—or him. "I think it's real beautiful. She wants to write poetry."

"More power to you," Ronda said, smiling at me. She really had a pretty smile.

Mr. Bixler was just staring at me. "But . . . you're sure you want to do this?" he asked.

I nodded.

And I wished he'd stop making such a scene about it! Didn't he think kids could write poetry, too?

"All right, then, if you're sure," Mr. Bixler said. "Welcome to the class."

Gee. Some welcome for his prize pupil.

"Well, then," Mr. Bixler said, finally not looking at me but looking around at the class. "Well, then, in this class we'll be exploring feelings, the feelings of published authors and poets such as the one I just read, as well as your own feelings expressed in poetry. I would like you, when you write, to express not only experiences but most of all, your feelings. And what I read earlier is a reminder that the absence of judgement helps us appreciate reality. Listen to your classmate's writing with an open heart. Now, who wants to go first?"

Betty spoke up. "I wrote a poem, but my son spilled tomato rice soup on it."

Charles muttered, "Yeah. Right."

"Well, it's true!" Betty said, and her face got all red.

Ray raised his hand. "I got one!" he said, and he stood up and began reading. "I sang a song for you to hear, I painted a picture for you to see, I picked a rose for you to smell, I planted grass for you to touch. But you did not hear my song. You did not see my picture. You did not smell my rose. You did not touch my grass."

Old Mrs. Hunsacker spoke up. "Maybe she was out of town," she said.

Who was out of town? I wondered.

And for some reason that seemed to make Charles mad. "That's not funny," he said. "His poem is about futility. We toil in unrewarded obscurity."

"Speak for yourself!" Mrs. Hunsacker said. "I own a split level."

And what did *that* have to do with poetry? Gee, grownups are weird.

Charles must have thought so too, because he said, "You're such a spud!"

And Mr. Bixler said, "I hear judgment."

Gee! And this was supposed to be a writing class.

Ronda raised her hand. "I experienced something with my boyfriend the other day. And I wrote down a few words."

Mr. Bixler smiled.

"Good," he said. "The floor is all yours."

He sat down, and Ronda stood up. She pulled her skirt down and smoothed it, then smoothed her shirt.

She began to read, in a sweet, low, breathy voice, like people do in love scenes in the movies.

Wow! It didn't matter *what* she wrote, if she could talk like that.

She said, "He protects me like a blanket from the cold dark night. As I look into his eyes, I know it's right. . . ."

She went on and on.

I looked around.

Was she *allowed* to be saying this?

But everyone was just nodding and smiling at her, and no one seemed embarrassed but me. Well, me and Mrs. Hunsacker. Mrs. Hunsacker's face and neck were very red. Even her ears were red.

Ronda finally ended the poem saying, "'I can't fight it. There's no point.'"

I looked at Mrs. Hunsacker again.

She was fanning herself.

Then I looked at Mr. Bixler. I wondered if he was going to yell at Ronda.

But he just smiled. "I'm glad you're willing to express yourself," he said. But his voice was kind of flat, and I couldn't tell at all what he was really thinking.

A couple more people raised their hands and read, and Mr. Bixler talked some more.

Finally I got up my courage and raised my hand.

"Yes, Vada?"

"I wrote a poem, too," I said.

"I'm glad!" Mr. Bixler said. And he made a motion for me to stand up, and he sat down.

I stood up. "'Ode to Ice Cream,' by Vada Sultenfuss," I said. "'I like ice cream a whole lot, It tastes good on days that are hot. On a cone or in a dish, this would be my only wish. Vanilla, chocolate, or rocky road, Even with pie à la mode.'"

I looked up. "That's all I have so far," I said.

Mr. Bixler said, "Vada, you know, it's sweet and all. Very sweet. But . . ."

"Sweet," Charles said. "Like ice cream?"

Mr. Bixler laughed. "No pun intended. But Vada, next time I want you to try to express what's in your soul. Your dreams. Your hopes."

My hopes? *That you'll wait for me to grow up.*

But I sure wasn't going to express that!

"Yeah," said Ronda. "In poetry you have to tell

how you see the world—your fears, your dreams, your innermost secrets."

"Secrets?" I said.

"Secrets," Justin said.

Everybody was looking at me, like they expected me to say a new poem right there on the spot, tell about all my secrets.

I could feel my face getting hot. Wow. If I had to tell real secrets . . .

I took Shelly's thirty-five dollars. And worse secrets. Much worse.

"Only the secrets you want to share," Mr. Bixler said quietly, looking at me like he knew I was worried. "In this class, we share only what we *can* share."

Whew! I sat down, relieved.

Good thing, or I'd never be a poet. How could I write about the really big secret? That I'm afraid I might have killed my mother.

_____ **CHAPTER**

X

The next morning I spent a lot of time writing a poem for next week's class. And then I had an idea. Dad is always writing death notices to put in the papers when people die. Since I was taking a writing class now, maybe I'd be good enough to help him! He'd be real proud of me if I could do that. But I wasn't going to tell him about taking the class, of course, 'cause then he'd need to know where the money came from.

I _would_ pay it back.

I ran downstairs to his little office.

He wasn't there, but suddenly I heard music coming from the kitchen—not radio music, real music.

His tuba! I haven't heard him play that since . . . well, since ages ago, when he used to play and Gramoo and me and Uncle Phil would dance and sing. And then I heard him singing, just like he used to. "Harry's wild about me!" he sang.

Wow! Was Gramoo better? Was she talking?

I raced down the hall to the kitchen, but stopped short outside. Because the music had stopped, and I could hear Dad and Shelly talking—and they were talking about *me!*

First thing I heard was Dad saying, ". . . want to apologize for the other day about Vada."

About *me?* What about me?

There was a silence, and then Dad went on. "I guess I was a little harsh, practically telling you outright to mind your business."

I crept closer to the door.

"No," Shelly said, "I shouldn't be sticking my nose into other people's business. It's just that I like Vada so much."

She does? I like her, too. But what had she done?

I peeked around the edge of the door.

Shelly was standing just inside the door, a newspaper in her hand.

Dad was across the room, sitting cross-legged on the floor in front of Gramoo, his tuba in his lap.

As I watched, he stood up, put the tuba down, and began patting Gramoo's hair.

But just like always, Gramoo acted like there was no one there at all.

That didn't stop Dad. He just kept patting and patting.

"See," he said, looking down at Gramoo, but talking to Shelly over his shoulder. "After my wife died, Gramoo moved in to care for Vada. They were

very close. Gramoo was just like a mother to Vada.
But lately, as Gramoo's mind is wandering more and
more, Vada's changing. She's always thinking she's
sick. And . . ."

Dad's voice trailed off.

"I think it's just that she's confused about death,"
Shelly said. "Maybe growing up in a funeral home."

Dad shook his head. "No, it wasn't until Gramoo
got sick that Vada started acting crazy."

Crazy! I have not been acting crazy.

And I hated having them talk about me like this.

But if I coughed or something, they'd be mad at me
for eavesdropping.

"She'll snap out of it," Dad said.

"She will," Shelly said.

Who? Gramoo? Or me?

Did he mean I wasn't really sick? But I *am* sick. I
mean, I hope he's right, but if my mom died and . . .

It was just too confusing. Maybe Shelly was right.
Maybe I *was* confused about death, but I didn't think
so. It's just that I keep getting sick. And that's not
pretend or confused. That's real.

Dad turned to face Shelly.

I started to back up farther. I didn't want them to
turn around and catch me there.

"Well," Shelly said after a minute. She wiggled the
newspaper. "I was just looking at the movie schedule.
I love movies, don't you? There's a revival of *Love
Story*. I saw that, cried my eyes out."

"I haven't been to a movie since . . ." Dad paused.
"In ages," he said softly.

"Oh, I love movies," Shelly said. "The drive-in,

especially. I don't think there's anything more romantic than being at a drive-in in your convertible on a breezy summer evening with that someone special, looking up at the stars." Her voice got dreamy-sounding, like it had the other day when she talked about love stories. "With someone special," she said again.

There was a long silence.

Then Dad said, "Someone special."

Shelly nodded. She took a few steps closer to Dad.

"You smell good," she said, sniffing. "What are you wearing?"

Dad just shrugged. "Formaldehyde?" he said.

They both laughed.

They just stood there looking at each other then—I mean, really *looking* at each other, into each other's eyes. And I could tell Dad wasn't thinking about me at all anymore.

Suddenly I had a scared feeling, because I knew where I'd seen that look before, or one a lot like it—on the covers of Shelly's love stories.

They seemed to stand there forever.

Then suddenly Dad turned away from her. He bent and put his tuba back in the case, fiddling with it to get it to fit right.

"Well," Shelly said finally, "I guess I'll go back to work."

Dad didn't answer.

She started for the door, and I fled for the stairs.

But as I did, I heard Dad say, "But I do like playing bingo. I go every week. You could come with me on my next bingo night. If you'd like."

She could go? And he'd never let *me* go, in all the times I've asked!

"I'd like," Shelly said.

"It's a deal," Dad said.

"A date," Shelly said quietly.

I fled up the stairs. He is so mean! Ask Shelly, but leave his own daughter home! I did not want him going out with Shelly. I mean, I like her and all, but I did not want him liking her—not liking her so much that he wanted to be with her and not me.

I ran to my room to work on a plan. I couldn't believe he'd let his own daughter stay home, when he let practically a stranger come with him. If he had any heart at all, he'd let me come. But just in case he didn't—either have a heart or let me come—by next bingo night I'd have a plan to stop this date.

*I*t was almost a week till the next bingo, and there was another writing class first. I thought of writing about Dad and Shelly and bingo, but decided no. It wasn't anyone's business, especially if I had to read it out loud. So I finished my poem about ice cream, and added some feelings—how I felt when I was eating ice cream and how I felt when I was finished. Like, cold. And sad because I wanted more.

I hoped that would satisfy them.

I got to the college early, but I didn't mill around with any of the people before class. Instead, I went and hid out in the bathroom till class time. I didn't think I wanted to talk to the old people, especially Mrs. Hunsacker. And Ronda seemed nice, but her poem had made me nervous.

I had a feeling Daddy wouldn't like me doing this too much.

Finally, when it was time for class to start, I went in and sat down. And that's when Mr. Bixler said, "Why don't we have class outside there under the trees?"

He pointed to the place just outside the door.

Wow! Class outside. He never let *our* class do that.

So we all trooped outside and sat in a circle on the grass and we took turns reading our poetry.

People had been busy writing all week. I couldn't believe how many people had written poems. But most of the poems I didn't understand, and the ones I did were pretty boring.

In fact, the whole class was kind of long and boring.

My poem had more feelings in it, but when it was my turn, I said I wanted to pass.

Mrs. Hunsacker had said that, and Mr. Bixler said fine.

It wasn't that I didn't really want to read. It was just that I was afraid people would start bugging me about how I should reveal more secrets.

But finally we got to the best part—when it was Mr. Bixler's turn to read.

I could just listen to him forever.

"I have something from a famous poet here," he said, smiling. "I'd like to share it with you."

He leaned against a tree and read softly: "'A thing of beauty is a joy forever: Its loveliness increases; it will never pass into nothingness; but still will keep a bower quiet for us, and a sleep full of sweet dreams, and health, and quiet breathing.'"

He looked over the class, smiling at us, his eyebrows raised.

What a smile!

I definitely hoped he'd wait for me to grow up.

"What do you think the poet is saying here?" he asked.

Charles spoke up. He has a very whiny kind of voice. I bet he was the kind of kid who had no friends when he was in school. "Well!" He cleared his throat. "Obviously Keats is saying that everything that is good never dies."

"No!" Ray said. "He means things die, but not their memory."

"People die," I said. "I've seen them."

Mr. Bixler smiled at me. "Yes," he said. "But Keats was exploring what happens *after* they die."

"They come to my house," I said.

Charles laughed and then tried to cover it up with a cough.

I made a face at him.

Mrs. Hunsacker raised her hand.

"Yes?" Mr. Bixler said.

"It's time to go," Mrs. Hunsacker said.

"Thank you. But first Ronda and Justin have asked if they could lead the class in group meditation."

Meditation? What was that?

Justin was right next to me, and he stood up. "This is really very cool," he said. "Okay, this is what you do—you send out your vibes to the group. Now get into this meditation position."

He sat down next to me and crossed his legs like he was a Buddha or someone doing breathing exercises on TV.

It wasn't hard to do, but a lot of people, like Mrs. Hunsacker, couldn't get their legs crossed like that.

Mrs. Hunsacker had on a skirt, too, so she was having trouble getting it tucked between her legs.

Finally she gave up and just knelt there like she was in church, praying.

When everyone was pretty much set, Ronda said, "Now everyone hold hands. You should try to feel what the other person is feeling without speaking any words."

Everybody took everybody else's hands.

I wished I'd gotten next to Mr. Bixler. But he had Betty and Ray.

I had Justin and Ronda.

I took their hands.

"Now close your eyes," Ronda said, in that low, breathy voice. "Close your eyes and breathe easily."

I closed my eyes—after I saw that everyone else did.

Weird. This was definitely the weirdest class I'd ever been in.

Justin began talking. "Send out your vibes," he said quietly. "Receive the others' at the same time. Can you all feel it?"

I didn't feel anything, except that it felt weird sitting there in the middle of a bunch of strangers with my eyes closed. It was a little bit like sleeping on a bus.

I opened my eyes, and peeked.

Everybody else's eyes were closed, even Mr. Bixler's. He looked kind of cute with his eyes closed.

There was a long silence. I kept looking at everybody.

Mrs. Hunsacker's eyelids were twitching, like she was asleep and dreaming in there.

"Okay, open your eyes," Ronda said quietly. "But keep on holding hands."

All the others opened their eyes. I pretended to be blinking at the light.

Justin's hand was getting sweaty, and he had a hangnail that was rough. I wanted to drop his hand so I could wipe away his sweat, but everyone else was still holding on.

"What did you feel?" Justin asked nobody in particular.

Ray said, "I felt Mrs. Hunsacker's strength."

Strength? Mrs. Hunsacker looked pretty old and weak to me.

"I felt something," Charles said. "I felt that Ronda is one with the earth. She's so cosmically in tune!"

What did *that* mean? I looked at Ronda, wondering if she knew or if she'd be insulted.

But all she said was, "Right! That's exactly what I sent out. And I felt you were full of peace and inner harmony."

Charles? Peace? He looked like a nervous wreck.

Mr. Bixler was smiling at me. "What did you feel, Vada?" he asked. "Anything special?"

I wanted to say I felt Justin's hangnail. But I knew that wasn't what they meant.

I just shrugged, and Mr. Bixler winked at me, like he and I had some secret.

I wondered if he didn't feel anything, either.

Justin dropped my hand, and everyone else dropped hands, too.

"Well, Vada," Justin said. "Next time, try to feel

something—something significant coming from the person."

A hangnail is significant, I thought. Gramoo once had a hangnail on her big toe that got infected, and the doctor had to slice it off her. I don't think Gramoo thought it was insignificant.

But I really knew that wasn't what he meant.

But I also knew I didn't feel anything. Except a hangnail and a sweaty hand.

"We'll do it again someday," Ronda said, addressing the whole group. "And don't worry, Vada. You'll catch on. You'll be able to send out and receive other people's messages very soon. It takes a bit of practice for some people, concentration. But it's so worth doing. You can get messages totally without words."

And that's when I had a terrific thought, something I could do. If it really worked.

We all collected out notebooks and stuff then and headed home.

I waited till night, when the whole house was quiet and everybody was asleep. Then I tiptoed down the hall to Gramoo's bedroom.

With the moonlight coming in the window, I could see Gramoo there in bed, lying flat on her back, her head on the pillow, her arms outside the covers, stiff-looking, almost the way they fix up the dead people.

Silently I climbed up on the foot of the bed and sat down, my legs crossed in that meditation position. I took Gramoo's hand quietly and sat for a long time, sending her all the messages I'd been wanting to give her for a long time.

But even though I sat quietly for a very long time, I didn't feel any messages coming back. But if she got mine, well, maybe in the morning she'd know what I was telling her. That I wanted her back. I needed her back with me. I missed her so much.

*N*ext morning Gramoo didn't seem much different, even though I watched her closely. But I was busy with other stuff, too, and I didn't have much time to just sit and watch, to see if she had gotten my messages. It was Dad's bingo day. And I had come up with not one, but two plans—plan A and, in case that didn't work, plan B. I called Thomas J and told him to be ready just in case I needed him for back-up plan B.

That night I planted myself right in the middle of the porch steps, so Dad had to practically walk over me to go to bingo. It was almost dark when he finally came out of the house.

He was all dressed up—a nice sports jacket and his good shoes—and he even had on some after-shave stuff that smelled nice, not like formaldehyde from a funeral parlor.

"Hey, Vada," he said, as he came down the steps. He tipped his head back and looked up at the stars. "Nice night, huh?"

"How come you're all dressed up just to play bingo?" I said.

Dad shrugged. "Just want to look nice."

"How come?" I said. "You never cared before."

Dad didn't answer. He kept looking at the stars.

"And you're wearing smelly stuff, too," I said.

"It's not smelly stuff," Dad said, laughing. "It's Old Spice."

"Well, how come you're wearing it, then?" I asked.

"Look, Vada." Dad sighed. "Look, Vada, Shelly's coming over and we're going to bingo together."

"Shelly?" I pretended to be surprised. "How come?"

"She likes to play bingo," Dad said.

I was about to say, She does not, she likes to go to drive-in movies—but then he'd know I'd been snooping.

I stood up. "I'll go with you, then," I said. "Both of us! Okay?"

Dad shook his head. "No, no, I don't think so," he said.

"Why not?"

"Well, it's just . . ."

"It's not a *date*, is it?" I said. I made the word "date" sound like something that smelled bad.

"Not a date, no. Not exactly."

"Then I can come."

Dad shook his head and sighed. "Look, Vada, you

stay home here with Gramoo, all right? I've told you, this is my one night out. In a week or so the fair will come to town and I'll take you to that. Okay?"

He didn't wait for my answer.

He just reached over and kissed the top of my head, then patted my hair. "Umm, smells good," he whispered.

And then he went down the steps and over to where his car was parked at the curb.

I was going to yell, So you like her better than me! But I didn't. I had more dignity. And a backup plan, too.

As I watched, Shelly pulled up in her camper. She got out and waved to me.

Then she got in the car with Dad.

I didn't wave back.

As soon as they were gone, I raced for Thomas J's house and around the back where his room is.

There was a light on in his room, and I stood under the window.

"Thomas J!" I called softly. "Hey, Thomas J."

In just a second his head appeared in the window.

"You ready?" I called.

"What if I get in trouble?" he whispered.

"You're not going to get in trouble," I said. "Just get out here."

His head disappeared from the window, and his light went out.

I ran to the back door where I knew he'd come out and crouched down by the garbage pails, hidden in the shadows.

In just a second the back door opened very quietly and Thomas J came out on the porch and down the steps.

"Vada?" he said softly.

I stepped out of the shadows. "Hey!" I said.

He clutched his throat. "Don't *do* that!" he whispered.

"Sorry," I said.

"I'm going to get in trouble if they know I'm out," Thomas J said. "I get asthma from the dark."

"Wimp!" I said.

"Am not!"

"Bed wetter!" I said.

"I stopped that!" he said.

"Then come on. We're going to the church hall to play bingo."

"But what if . . ."

I ran away, and he chased after me. I knew he would.

When he caught up to me, he said, "They're not going to let us in, Vada, we're kids! And I don't even like to play bingo."

"We're not playing, we're watching. Come on. This is important."

We ran all the way to the church hall. They always set up a big tent for bingo and Thomas J and I went to the tent door and peeked in. People were already playing. We crouched down behind the tent flap, peeking up just enough to see but not be seen. I hoped.

Dad and Shelly had a table in the back, right near us. They were so close that if I stood up and leaned out, I could almost read their cards. We couldn't hear exactly what they said with all the noise, but I heard Shelly say something about putting makeup on people and Dad talking about his "strategy" for bingo. Boring.

Most of the people in the tent looked to be about a hundred years old, including the people at Dad's table. One of the couples at Dad's table were Mr. and Mrs. Swope from our church. Mr. and Mrs. Swope were not only super old, they were also super deaf.

"Hey!" Thomas J said suddenly, pointing. "There's your dad and Shelly."

I shoved his hand down.

"Shhh. I don't want them to know I'm here. What do you think we're hiding for?"

"We going to stay here all night?" Thomas J said.

I didn't answer.

"This is boring!" Thomas J said.

"Hush!" I whispered.

The announcer was already calling out numbers, and people were putting chips on their cards.

But I noticed that at Dad's table, the old ladies were only halfway playing their cards. Mostly they were staring at Dad and Shelly.

Staring just like me—because Dad and Shelly were acting like jerks. Shelly kept blinking up at Dad, inching closer to him, like she wanted to get inside his pocket. And Dad, he was wiggling a bit, like he was uncomfortable and wanted to get away. But I noticed he didn't move very far.

Every time the announcer called a number, Mr. Swope poked Mrs. Swope, reminding her to look at her card.

"What?" she yelled once.

"C-nineteen!" he yelled back.

But Mrs. Swope and the other old lady were staring so hard that Dad finally noticed.

He looked up from his card and nodded at her. " 'Evening," he said. "Nice night, isn't it, Mrs. Swope?"

Mrs. Swope turned to her husband.

"What'd he say?" she shouted.

I looked at Thomas J and he looked at me, and I thought we'd die, we were both trying so hard not to laugh.

Thomas J slid down to the ground gasping, he was laughing so hard.

But I stayed standing. I didn't want to miss anything.

"Can we go yet?" Thomas J said, from the ground at my feet. "It's boring just watching."

"You go!" I whispered. "I'm staying."

"You know I can't go alone," Thomas J said. "I'm not allowed to go out by myself after dark, and you know it." He was tugging at the rubber around the soles of his sneakers. "Why'd you want me here anyway if we weren't going to play?"

"You know why," I said.

"Why?"

"Because we're blood brothers. We do everything together, don't we? Now shush."

I was watching Dad. And Shelly. She was getting closer and closer to Dad.

I swear she was going to kiss him. Right there in front of everybody. She was going to do it!

And he wasn't doing anything to stop her.

Now the old people were *really* staring—Mr. and Mrs. Swope and the others, too.

The announcer called, "F-eleven!"

And Shelly leaned close to Dad, looking up into his face. Dad leaned close to her, a look on his face like on that book jacket, like he was about to kiss her right there in front of everyone.

I jumped up. "Bingo!" I yelled.

Thomas J jumped up, too, and stared at me.

"We have a winner!" the announcer yelled.

"There was no bingo. That came from outside," Mr. Swope yelled.

Thomas J and I both jumped back.

"How did someone outside get a bingo?" another old guy said.

"Someone outside didn't get a bingo," Mr. Swope said. "Someone outside *yelled* bingo, you moron."

"Who are you calling a moron?" the old guy yelled.

"Vernon, put a lid on it," Mrs. Swope said.

Thomas J and I had our hands over our mouths, we were trying so hard not to laugh out loud.

But Thomas J was wide-eyed, too, like he was scared.

"Would the winner please raise their hand?" the announcer said.

Uh-oh.

Nobody did.

"See!" Vernon yelled. He was really mad by then. "And I won't put a lid on it. If that guy wasn't two hundred years old, I'd . . ."

Suddenly the other old man lunged across the table.

He and Mr. Swope started clawing at each other madly.

Their wives were frantically trying to pull them apart.

But the wives were no match for them, and the two old guys were hammering at each other.

Dad was yelling, "Fellas, fellas, it's just bingo, fellas. . . ."

And Thomas J and I were hysterical.

In a minute Dad and Shelly got up and got into it. Dad had a hold of one old guy, and Shelly got her arms around Mr. Swope.

Shelly and Dad were pulling hard at them, backing them off each other.

It was a complete uproar.

And nobody was looking into anyone's eyes anymore.

I turned to Thomas J, smiling.

"Okay," I whispered. "We can go now."

I waited up till Dad and Shelly got home that night, sitting with my chin propped up on the windowsill in my room. I waited a long, long time, but they didn't come back. Eventually I finally fell asleep that way, sitting right up in the chair, my chin on the window ledge.

I don't know what woke me up—if it was just my stiff neck or that my legs were asleep or what. Maybe it was because in my sleep, I heard them. All I know is that when I woke up, there were Shelly and Dad outside on the street—Shelly and Dad in the street, right in front of Shelly's camper. Dancing.

Dancing! In the middle of the street in the dark.

I could hear music coming from someplace, probably Shelly's camper, and a small light shining on them, streaming out from the camper door.

Darn! I should have stayed up, sat on the porch all night till they came home.

They danced and danced, Dad's arms wrapped tight around Shelly, her looking up into his face.

From my room I couldn't see the look on her face, but I bet I knew—all moony, goopy, like she'd looked back at the bingo tent.

Then, as I watched, Dad kissed her. He put his face right down to hers and kissed her. On the mouth, too.

They stayed in each other's arms for a long time.

I wished Gramoo was awake—that she'd start bellowing out one of her songs. That would stop them.

Watching them like that made me feel less bad about borrowing Shelly's money. She shouldn't have come here in the first place.

After a minute I heard Shelly's clock yell "cuckoo!" And like that was a signal or something, Shelly and Dad moved away from each other.

Had I known, I would have yelled "cuckoo!" long ago.

Then I could see they were talking, but I couldn't hear what they said. And then another kiss—but a short one this time—and Dad came up to the porch and Shelly went into her camper.

But I watched Dad stand on the porch for a minute, watching till Shelly's camper pulled away, and I heard them call good night.

Disgusting. Grown-ups shouldn't act like that.

I had to come up with a plan, make something happen—make her have a rainy day so she'd have to leave. But what?

I didn't know, but I knew I'd come up with something.

Next morning I was on my way out to find Thomas J, when I went past the downstairs bathroom.

The door was open, and Shelly was standing in front of the mirror, putting on lipstick.

I stopped and watched her, my hands on my hips. I knew what she was doing. And why.

"You going out somewhere?" I asked.

"Nope," she answered. She applied more lipstick and some lip pencil kind of thing.

"So how come you're putting lipstick on?"

"A woman's got to look her best," Shelly said, frowning at herself in the mirror. "At all times."

Ha! For my dad, you mean.

"Well, I think lipstick looks fake," I said. "Very."

Shelly smiled at me. "Ever tried any?"

"No."

Shelly put the lid down on the toilet. She pointed. "Here, sit down."

"Why?" I said.

"Just sit."

I did. I don't know why. I knew she was going to put lipstick on me, and I knew it was stupid. And I was also mad at her. But for some weird reason I sat.

"Give me your face," she said, putting her hand under my chin and tilting my face up.

I wasn't sure I was going to like this. But then, maybe if I wore lipstick, if I looked pretty like Shelly, Dad would let me come to bingo games, too.

Shelly put stuff on my lips. It felt slimy, and I scrunched up my face.

"Quit wiggling," she said. "I'm going to miss your mouth."

She worked on me awhile, then stood back and looked at me, then handed me a piece of tissue.

"Blot your lips."

I did.

Shelly tilted her head and looked at me. "It looks really pretty on you," she said.

I licked my lips. "It tastes funny."

"You're not supposed to eat it," Shelly said. "Now close your eyes. I want to bring out those gorgeous blue eyes of yours."

She began putting stuff on my eyes.

"The first rule to remember in applying makeup," she said, "is that you can never wear enough blue eye shadow."

"Do you like putting makeup on people?" I asked.

"Yes. I've been trying to get to Hollywood for years now so I could do makeup for all the movie stars. But I haven't gotten there yet."

Well, I thought, maybe you will. Maybe we should try to find you a job out there.

But all I said was "I wouldn't worry about it too much. I've heard they're difficult to work with, movie stars."

Shelly laughed. "Now open your eyes," she said. "Open them and have a look."

I did. I stood up and looked in the mirror.

I looked like a raccoon. Or a prizefighter who had lost. Or . . .

But it was . . . well, different. I definitely looked grown up. Weird grown up. But grown up.

I tipped my head from side to side, looking at myself in the mirror. "Shelly, do you think I'm pretty?"

"Oh, yes!" Shelly said. "Very pretty. You've got great big sparkling eyes and the cutest nose. And I love your cute little haircut. You have . . . style!"

"The boys at school don't think so," I said.

"What do they know?" she said. "You just wait. They'll come around. And what about Thomas J? He thinks so, doesn't he?"

I shrugged. "Thomas J isn't a boy. Well, he's a boy, but not a boyfriend kind of boy."

"Well, you're very pretty," Shelly said.

"Do you have to be pretty to have a guy like you?" I asked.

She smiled. "It helps."

"You like my dad, don't you?" I asked.

"He's all right," she said.

But in the mirror I could see that she was blushing.

"I don't think he likes you," I said.

"You don't?" she said. "Why not?"

"Well, I mean, he likes you okay. But he's nice to everyone. It's not that you're . . . special or anything."

"Oh," she said. But I thought that she was smiling.

And then I could feel myself blushing.

Why was I such a nerd? She could see what I was doing—trying to do. And she probably thought I was a big baby.

"You like the makeup?" she said.

I started to say yes, I do, because I did, kind of.

But then I remembered that I was mad at her.

So instead I just said, "Shelly, I'd definitely hold off on that Hollywood thing."

A few minutes later I was going through the hall to go outside when I heard Shelly talking to someone. Who?

Dad?

I tiptoed back to the kitchen–family room. It's true I was spying, but I didn't care. I needed to see how they were acting to each other.

But there was no Dad—just Shelly kneeling beside Gramoo, talking to her just the way I do. The way I try to.

"How are you doing today, Mrs. Sultenfuss?" Shelly said quietly.

And then, when Gramoo just kept staring and rocking, Shelly went on. "You should talk to Vada," she said. "It would do her a world of good."

CHAPTER

XIV

Next day I found some of Shelly's makeup and tried putting it on myself.

I didn't know if I did good or not—to me, it looked a little weird, especially my eyes. They looked kind of bruised. But I remembered what Shelly had said—a girl can never wear too much blue eye shadow. And my lips were . . . well, red.

I went outside and found Thomas J sitting on the grass beside the house.

"Your lip bleeding?" he said.

I made a face at him. "No."

He frowned. "You don't look good. Your eyes are . . ."

"A girl can never wear enough blue eye shadow," I said.

"Oh," Thomas J said. He shrugged and picked up his bike. "Where's your bike?" he asked.

"In the garage. Give me a ride."

I hopped on the back of his bike, and he started toward the garage, wobbling all over the place. He really isn't very strong. But eventually we got going after I gave us a little push along the ground.

The garage is a mess, an even worse mess than my room. There's stuff everywhere—boxes of clothes and boxes with Gramoo's hobby and craft stuff, her sewing and bird-watching stuff and her stamp collections and photo albums. Gramoo collects—used to collect—almost as much junk as Thomas J. And when she got tired of one hobby, she brought it out to the garage and started in on a new one.

I picked up my bike, but then looked down at the handlebars. One of the streamers was missing.

"My streamer," I said. "It's gone. Help me look. It must be around here somewhere."

I got down on my hands and knees, and Thomas J did, too. We crept around the floor, looking.

But after a minute Thomas J crawled off into a corner.

"You're not helping!" I said.

"But look what I found!" I said. And he held up a plastic skull, all marked up with lines and words.

"That was Gramoo's," I said, laughing. "It's a phrenology chart."

I had forgotten about that hobby. Gramoo used to tell people what their personalities were like by feeling the bumps on their heads. She even did it to dead people a few times till Dad made her stop. That was right before she got really weird.

"What'd she have it for?" Thomas J said.

"Phrenology," I said. "People used to study the bumps in your head to see if you had a good personality. Bring it here. I'll diagnose your head."

"No," he said, backing up.

"Come on. It's fun."

"Does it hurt?"

I just made a face at him.

He made a face back, but slowly he came over to me and handed me the skull.

"Sit!" I said, "Backwards."

He did—sat in front of me cross-legged, his back to me.

Slowly, carefully, I slid my hands over his skull.

Gosh, he had a skinny little head!

"Hmm," I said. I deliberately made my voice thoughtful-sounding, like I had discovered something important. "Very interesting."

"What?" Thomas J said.

"Sad," I said.

"What?" he said.

"You have no personality," I said. "None at all."

He turned around and grabbed for the plastic head. "I want to see where it says that," he said.

I grabbed back.

We fell over and knocked over some small boxes. And surprisingly Thomas J ended up with the skull.

I got up and went to straighten up the boxes. One of them was stamp books, and one of them was pictures.

I scooped up the pictures to stuff them back in. I didn't want to wreck Gramoo's hobbies, because when she got better she might want them.

As I was stuffing the pictures back in a box, suddenly I saw a picture of Dad—Dad looking lots younger, but still definitely him. He was standing in front of an old-fashioned-looking car—with a woman.

My mother.

I've seen her before in pictures—Dad has some around, and Gramoo used to show me many pictures of her—but it's always sort of a surprise to see a new picture.

"Who's that with your dad?" Thomas J said, looking over my shoulder. "Your mom?"

"Yes. My mother."

Thomas J sat down next to me. "Do you remember her?" he asked.

"No."

"Where do you think she is?"

"Gramoo says she's in heaven."

"What do you think it's like?"

"What?"

"Heaven."

"I think . . ."

What did I think? Well, that no one was sick in heaven. And that they never were afraid. And you never got this feeling like this thing was stuck in your throat. And you got whatever you wanted, like . . . But was it too weird to say those things?

But Thomas J was looking at me, like he wanted to know, really.

"Well," I said slowly, "I think that everyone gets their own horse or their own bike or car or whatever it is they like to ride. And all they do is ride them and eat whatever they want all day long. And everybody is best friends with everybody else, and when they play sports, there are no teams so no one gets picked last. And you don't have to be scared of that. Actually, nobody's scared of anything. And nobody has allergies or gets sick. And they take care of each other, like friends. And . . . and nobody has to die."

"What if you *are* afraid, though? Afraid to ride horses?" Thomas J asked.

"It doesn't matter," I said. "Because you don't *have* to ride if you don't want to. You don't have to do anything if you don't want to."

"But what if I wanted to ride but I was afraid to?"

I just shook my head at him.

What a weird kid! He was even worried about heaven!

I sighed. "It doesn't matter, see, because they're not regular horses. They got wings, and it's no big deal if you fall. You just land in a cloud."

"Doesn't sound so bad," Thomas J said.

He stood up then. "Come on, let's go. We'll never find your streamer."

I got up and got on my bike, and Thomas J did, too.

Thomas J rode out first. But before I left the garage, I picked up the picture of Dad and my mother standing in front of the car, smiling. I put the picture in my pocket. I was going to take it to my room, maybe put it under my pillow with the old one I had there.

My mother, smiling. My mother before I killed her.

Maybe later I could remind Dad of it, show it to him sometime. Maybe if he remembered her, he wouldn't want Shelly. And maybe someday I could even ask him if it *was* my fault.

But that wasn't the only reason I put it in my

pocket. I needed it for some other reason. I wasn't sure why, but I did. Maybe because of yesterday—Shelly and putting on makeup and stuff. Maybe because when you're getting old enough to put on lipstick and wear eye shadow, maybe then you didn't need your dad's girlfriend to show you how. Maybe you needed a mother, a real mother. Even if it was just a picture of one.

*T*hings got worse after that—much worse. Dad and Shelly acted lovey to each other all the time. Dad acted like he didn't even know I was around. Well, he always acts like I'm invisible, but it got worse. All he was thinking of was Shelly, I could tell. I even caught him looking at himself in mirrors, and he wore Old Spice *all* the time now.

We were getting ready for our usual Fourth of July picnic, but instead of just us—Dad and me and Uncle Phil and Gramoo—Dad had invited Shelly. Then one day when Dad and I were shopping for the picnic, we met Shelly in the supermarket, and Dad walked away from me to be with Shelly, and he went all around the store with her, like he had completely forgotten I was with him. So by accident, when I was trying to catch up with him, I ran the cart into his heel. And he turned and yelled at me, right there in front of Shelly, in front of everybody in the supermarket, like I had done it on purpose or something.

He apologized later, but I think that was only because he saw Shelly looking at him weird.

By the Fourth of July day, I was so mad I was hardly speaking to him.

Not that he noticed.

When it was finally night, and time for our picnic, Dad cooked hamburgers and hot dogs on the grill, and Shelly brought her potato salad—she called it her "famous De Voto potato salad."

Barf.

When we sat down for our supper outside, I raced to the picnic table to get next to Dad.

I sat so close I was practically in his lap.

Ha! Shelly had to sit next to Uncle Phil, across the table from us. Gramoo was at the end of the table, a little American flag in her lap that Shelly had brought for her. But Gramoo didn't seem to notice it was there. She just played with her fork until Dad fed her a little and she began to catch on.

When we were all seated, Shelly said to Dad, "I just *love* your apron."

"Thanks," Dad said, smiling. He looked down at his apron, and I thought he was blushing.

I rolled my eyes and looked at Uncle Phil.

He winked at me.

I picked up my hamburger and took a bite.

But Shelly bowed her head like she was going to pray. And then she said, "Rub-a-dub-dub. Thanks for the grub."

"Hey, that's good!" Dad said, laughing.

Again I looked at Uncle Phil. Again he winked at me.

I chewed my hamburger awhile. Then I looked at Shelly.

"Hey, Shelly," I said. "You like seafood?"

"Sure," she said, smiling across the table at me.

I opened my mouth wide and showed her a mouthful of chewed-up food.

"See? Food," I said.

"That's attractive," she said.

"Va-da!" Dad said.

No sense of humor at all. None.

I looked up and noticed a car coming down the street, very slowly. It passed our house, then turned around and came back and stopped out front.

Uh-oh. Someone needing Dad, I bet. Well, good. He could go take care of them, and I wouldn't have to watch him and Shelly making eyes at each other.

But I felt bad, too, because I didn't want him to miss the fireworks.

"Dad?" I said. "There's a car just parked out front."

Dad shook his head and muttered under his breath, "Always happens. Always."

And he started to wipe his mouth and put on his serious look.

Just then two men came around the house and into the backyard. They looked alike, both tall and dark and kind of slimy-looking. But one was super thin, sort of like Charles in the poetry class, and the other was a little softer and fatter, especially around his stomach.

Shelly jumped up. "Stay here!" she said. "I'll be right back. They're for me."

She dropped her napkin and went up to the two guys. "What are you doing here?" she asked. Even though I could tell she was speaking through her teeth, her voice came through clear—and mad. Boy, was she mad!

"Mutual assets," the skinny guy said. "Does that ring a bell?"

"How did you find me?" Shelly said.

Find her? Oh, good! They were cops. Come to get her!

"You told everyone where you were going. I'm here for the motor home." He sounded super mean when he spoke, like he was holding a gun just out of sight.

I felt my heart racing hard. So she was a thief! A car thief! And that money—the cookie-jar money. I bet she had stolen that, too!

Shelly had her hands on her hips and was tapping her foot.

I could have told her that was no way to treat a cop.

But she leaned in close to the skinny guy and said, "I bought it. I paid for it. And I've lived in it for over a year. The camper's mine!"

She *bought* it?

"Mutual asset," the skinny guy said. "That's what the lawyer called it. Not Shelly's recreational vehicle."

I looked at Dad and Uncle Phil.

Dad's eyes were screwed up tight and I've never seen him look so mean. Not even when he yelled at me in the supermarket the other day.

Uncle Phil was smiling a little. He leaned close to Dad. "I don't think those two have a good relationship," he said quietly.

"Can I eat Shelly's hot dog?" I said.

Dad didn't answer me. He stood up. He didn't leave the table, just stood there watching.

"Come on," Shelly said. "My boss is watching. I'd better introduce you."

She came back to the table, the two guys following her. She introduced us to Danny and Ralph. Danny was the skinny one. "And this is Harry, Phil, Gramoo and Vada Sultenfuss," she said.

"Vada Sultenfuss?" Danny said, shaking his head. "Tough break, kid."

"*I* like it!" I said.

"He's from Detroit," Shelly said, nodding her head in Danny's direction. "We used to be married."

Dad and Phil stood up and shook hands with the two men.

Dad looked at the guy named Danny—Shelly's husband. I could tell *that* was making him think.

"Are you here to take Shelly back?" I asked Danny.

"Nice to meet you, Mr. De Voto," Dad said to Danny. And he glared at me.

"Welcome to our little hamlet, Mr. De Voto," Uncle Phil said.

Little *hamlet?*

"We have burgers and hot dogs," Dad said. "I hope you'll join us."

"Can't stay," Danny said. "I'm only here because my wife—"

113

"Ex-wife!" Shelly said.

"My *ex*-wife seems to have ripped off my camper!" Danny said, sounding really angry.

"Shelly?" Dad said.

"Honestly, Harry," Shelly said. "He got the Mustang and the rent-controlled apartment. I promise you—"

"Oh, I don't think so," Danny said. "In fact, I have a copy of our property settlement here and . . ."

He pulled something out of his back pocket.

"Oh, nuts! This is my lease. How dumb can I be?"

He sank into a chair and began rubbing his forehead. "I keep forgetting things. I think I'm getting senile."

He looked over at Gramoo.

I went to stand beside her.

The guy named Ralph just stood there looking from Dad to Danny to Shelly, then back again, not saying a word. I wondered if he was deaf or mute or something.

Danny picked up a hamburger from the stack on a plate and began munching it. "And my stomach's a mess. I keep getting those attacks."

"Are you eating greasy foods again?" Shelly asked.

He looked down at the hamburger in his hand, then let it drop onto the table.

"My whole *life's* a mess," he said, rubbing his head again.

"Danny?" Dad said.

"What?"

"You're suffering a loss and there's little comfort one can offer. But I urge you to focus on the time you *had* with the camper. The trips you took, the sights you saw. Those days are over, but they will live forever in your heart."

Danny looked up at Shelly. "Is this guy for real? Are you and him—"

"That's a real bonehead thing to say," Shelly said. *Dad* sounded like the bonehead to me.

Danny stood up and tugged at Shelly's arm. "Give me the keys," he said.

Shelly pulled back, but Danny was holding tight. "Stop it!" Shelly said. "You're hurting me!"

Suddenly Dad moved around the table—fast. I've *never* seen him move that fast. Dad's fist shot out, and with one punch to the stomach, suddenly Danny was on his knees.

Ralph spoke up for the first time. "Hey, what'd you do that for?" he asked.

"Who are you?" Dad asked.

"Ralph. His brother."

"Then you'll probably be visiting here quite often," Dad said.

"What? Why?"

"Because if he *ever* tries to take that camper," Dad said, "I'm gonna bury him in the front yard."

Shelly and Uncle Phil and I just stared at Dad. Uncle Phil was smiling.

Ralph knelt down and bent over Danny.

Uncle Phil leaned close to me. "Your dad's a real savage," he whispered. But I could tell he was laughing.

Danny straightened up. "I can't believe you did that," he said. He sounded like he was crying.

"You were behaving badly," Dad said. "Want some supper?"

"I'm gettin' out of here," Danny said. "Come on, Ralph."

Danny and Ralph went out front, and all of us—all but Gramoo—trailed along behind. I wanted to be sure they didn't steal Shelly's camper. Because no matter how stupid things had been with Shelly, I didn't want her to have no place to live.

And then I had another terrible thought: if she lost her camper and had no place to live, she'd *have* to live with us. I had to be sure the camper stayed here.

When we got out front, Ralph got in the driver's side of the car, and Danny climbed in the other side.

"'Bye, Danny," Shelly said nicely, like she really was his friend. "And say hi to all my old friends."

"I never see those people," Danny said. "I don't think they ever really liked me."

Shelly leaned in and kissed Danny on the cheek, just a little peck.

Danny sighed. Then he gave a last look at Shelly and a last sad look at the camper. "Mutual asset," he whispered.

"Maybe he was talking about the dog," Shelly said. "How is Sidney anyway?"

"He's sick. He has colitis," Danny said.

"'Bye, Danny. See you, Ralph," Shelly said.

And we all watched as they drove away. Shelly turned to Dad. "That was pretty great," she said.

"Is it really your camper?" Dad asked.

She smiled and turned one hand first this way, then that. "Gray area."

"Did you love him?" Dad asked.

"Yes," Shelly said quietly. "I used to. I would never marry anyone I didn't love."

Then she and Dad were giving each other that *look* again.

Uncle Phil took my arm. "Come on. Give you a push on the swings," he said softly.

But I knew the real reason.

Still, I didn't want to stand and watch them, either, so I went with him to the yard. But I didn't want him to push me on the swing. I'm not a baby.

We went over to the table. Uncle Phil stood beside Gramoo and took her hand, stroking and holding it between both his own.

"He likes Shelly, doesn't he?" I said. "I never saw him hit anyone in his life."

"Yes," Uncle Phil answered. "He likes her."

"Does he love her, you think?"

"Probably."

"Do you like her?"

"Yes," Uncle Phil said. "And she's very good for your father."

"Why? Why 'good'?"

"After your mother died, your dad was sad all the time. But before that, he was really funny."

"Dad was?" I said. "Really?"

"When he's with Shelly, he sort of reminds me of the old Harry," Uncle Phil said.

"My dad was funny?"

"Well, he wasn't one of the Marx Brothers, but he made me laugh. You'd be surprised."

I would. Very surprised.

117

I found myself remembering something Gramoo said once. She said they told my mom that she'd never have children, and that I was a surprise.

Steven Wallace once put a spider down my back. I didn't like that surprise.

I didn't like surprises, period. I needed to know things right out—like what that thing is in my throat. And if Mr. Bixler liked me and would wait for me.

And I definitely didn't want any surprises from Dad.

CHAPTER

XVI

My throat hurt so much that night that the next morning I went to get Thomas J to go with me to see Dr. Welty.

When I called for Thomas J, his mother came out on the porch with him, her hand on his shoulder.

"Wait a minute," Mrs. Sennett said, holding him back. "I saw something." She turned him to face her and then licked her fingers and wiped his mouth. "You had a milk mustache," she said.

He made a face, but he smiled at his mom and she smiled back. And I thought for a minute that I wouldn't mind being him.

Mrs. Sennett smiled at me then. "Riding bikes?" she asked.

I nodded. I wasn't going to tell her we were going to Dr. Welty's. I wondered if Thomas J ever told her about that.

"Have fun, kids!" she said. And she went back in the house. Over her shoulder she called to Thomas J, "And your bed better be made."

"It is, it is," he muttered.

"Let's go," I said.

"To the lake?" he asked.

I shook my head. "To Dr. Welty."

He nodded. "You sick?" he asked.

"Yeah."

When we got to Dr. Welty's I left Thomas J in the waiting room, like always, and went in alone. After what Dr. Welty had said last week about Mr. Layton, I couldn't say that I thought I had a tumor, a cancer. So I just decided I'd tell him I felt like I had gotten a chicken bone stuck there at the picnic last night. Of course, he didn't need to know we hadn't had any chicken last night. But I needed him to check my throat at least once more. If the tumor had grown since last week and was going to choke me to death during the night, maybe by now Dr. Welty could see it.

But Dr. Welty just said there was no chicken bone in my throat.

"Everything's fine!" he said. And then he added, "How's Thomas J these days? Is he doing okay—his asthma?"

"He's right in the waiting room. Why don't you ask him? Are you sure I'm all right?"

"You're *fine*, Vada." He smiled at me. "Just fine."

Fine? Ha! It wasn't *his* father who was falling in love with Shelly.

I was just on my way out of the examining room when I heard Mrs. Randall talking to Thomas J. She was showing him how to put water in a syringe—a syringe that had no needle—and how to use it like a squirt gun.

Thomas J always surprises me. He can get *anyone* to do stuff with him—even grumpy old Mrs. Randall.

Thomas J held out the syringes. "Look what we got!" he said.

"I want one!" I said.

Thomas J handed me one of the two he had, and then, right there, he squirted me.

I chased him outside and squirted him back.

We got on our bikes, then headed down the street.

Without talking about it or anything, we ended up heading for the willow tree and the lake.

Thomas J was squirting everything in sight—trees, flowers, even a dog.

We came to the lake, and both of us stopped to refill at the edge of the lake.

When I came back to Thomas J, he was standing very still near a big oak tree, just looking up.

"What are you looking at?" I asked.

"There's a beehive up there."

"Where?"

He pointed with his syringe.

"So?"

He took aim and squirted.

"You're nuts!" I said. "You'll get stung."

"Stand back!" Thomas J said. "We'll chase them out of there, and then I can have the hive. I'll add it to my collection."

Weird. First he collects dead bugs and now bug houses.

He squirted again, but he didn't even hit it.

"That's stupid," I said, pushing him back. "You're going to get stung."

"Nah, we won't," Thomas J said.

He picked up a rock and threw it at the nest.

It missed, and the rock almost fell back on his head. He ducked.

"You're nuts!" I said. "What do you want it for, anyway?"

"'Cause they're neat," he said. "I have a wasps' nest, and now I'll have a beehive. Anyway, there are no bees around it. They swarm around if it's a live nest. I saw that when I got the wasps' nest. This is empty. And did you ever see inside a hive? It's really cool. There's a million separate spaces, like each bee has its own little tiny room."

"Thomas J," I said. "You are *too* weird. And we're both going to get stung."

He looked so sad that for a minute I felt sorry for him. And then I decided if he wanted the hive, I'd help him get it. Anyway, he was probably right about it being empty. There wasn't a bee in sight. Besides, knowing Thomas J's athletic ability—or lack of it—I was sure he'd never hit the hive by himself.

We both picked up rocks and threw.

I couldn't hit it for beans. I had almost as bad an aim as he did.

But finally, after a few more throws, Thomas J hit the hive—hit it hard—and the hive fell. A soft thump and it was right there on the ground in front of us.

We both jumped back, and I threw my arm in front

of Thomas J, holding him back like I was protecting him. What was I doing that for? Did I think I was his mother? Dummy. But I was sure that about a thousand bees would come swarming at us.

I didn't have to worry, though. Nothing happened. There were no bees in it at all.

Thomas J went closer and poked the hive with the toe of his sneaker.

No bees. He must have been right that it was an old hive, an empty one.

And then I looked down at my hand. My ring, my mood ring! It was gone!

"My ring!" I yelled. "It's gone." I got down on my hands and knees and began searching the grass. "Help me, Thomas J!" I said. "My ring. It's lost."

"Where'd it go?" he said.

"If I knew *where* . . . Oh, never mind. But I had it on. It must have come off when I was throwing!"

Thomas J got down on his hands and knees next to me. We both searched, patting the grass.

It wasn't there. And it was my favorite ring!

"I loved that ring!" I said. I felt close to tears.

"You'll find it," Thomas J said. "Don't worry. I'll help you."

Maybe it had fallen off at Dr. Welty's when Thomas J and I were chasing each other?

"Help! Watch it!" Thomas J yelled suddenly.

He grabbed my arm and yanked hard. "Run! They're alive."

I looked where he was looking. Bees, a million bees! They were swarming toward us from out of the hive, zillions of them, a whole black cloud of them.

"They're after us!" Thomas J yelled. He looked around wildly.

At that exact moment I saw my ring.

I reached for it just as the black cloud zoomed at my head.

Forget the ring!

"Run!" I shouted to Thomas J. "Run for your life!"

I jumped to my feet, and he did, too.

I raced for the water, the bees right above my head. "In the water!" I shouted. "In the lake."

"But I got my clothes on!" Thomas J shouted. He stopped at the edge of the water.

I didn't care what he did. I didn't stop to argue, either.

I just threw myself into the lake, clothes and shoes and all.

In just a second Thomas J splashed in next to me.

We stayed underwater as long as we could. When we came up, we didn't even speak for a few minutes. My heart was racing like mad.

Thomas J reached out and took my hand.

Together we crouched in the lake, just our eyes and noses above water, watching the bees at the edge of the lake, swarming and buzzing around like an angry cloud.

"They're not in the hive anymore," Thomas J said softly. "Later I can get it."

"Dork!" I said. "You could have gotten us both hurt bad."

"But the bees are out of it now," he said. "And we *didn't* get hurt." He sounded very smug.

"Right. And the bees are about to attack us if we come out of the water. We might have to stay here all day."

"Oh, no," Thomas J said. "I told my mother I'd be home for lunch."

A bee dive-bombed toward us, and we both ducked under.

When I came back up I said, "We better move farther out."

Thomas J looked nervous. "You know I can't swim."

"We don't have to get out over your head," I said.

We inched farther out, watching the swarming bees.

They seemed to have settled down around the hive, and they weren't looking for us anymore. But there were hundreds of them swarming back and forth between the tree and the hive. Some settled on top of it, some were just buzzing around.

"When it's empty, I'm going to go get it," Thomas J said.

"You're weird," I said.

But now what? We couldn't come out of the water yet. We might be stuck here for a long time.

Thomas J looked at me, as if he had had the same thought as I did. "Can we sit down?" he said.

I laughed. "If you can breathe."

We inched around in the water, getting closer to the edge where it wasn't so deep, keeping one eye on the bees.

When we were able to sit, we both did, just our heads sticking up.

"Vada?" he said. "How come you go to Dr. Welty's so much?"

"'Cause I'm sick!"

"What did Dr. Welty say before?" he asked.

"Nothing. You know him. He said I was fine."

"Are you?" he asked.

"No," I said.

"Are you dying, you think?"

It sounded weird, saying it out loud like that. I just shrugged.

Thomas J looked at me.

Water was dripping off his hair, and he looked even younger than he usually looks.

"Do *you* think I'm dying?" I asked.

"No," Thomas J said. "No."

For some reason, him saying that made me feel better than when Dr. Welty said it.

"But you know what I do think?" he said.

"What?" I said.

Because, funny—but I *did* want to know what he thought. I wondered myself sometimes why I was so sure that I was dying.

"I think you get scared of all those dead people in your house," Thomas J said. "And you know how they say if you can't beat them, join them? If you're one of them, then it's not so scary."

Wow. Thomas J thought that?

Could he be right? But I didn't think so. It was more than that, more than just having dead people around. But I didn't know what.

"Anyway," Thomas J said, "you're my best friend. I hope you don't die."

And you're *my* best friend, I thought.

But for some odd reason, I couldn't say it out loud. It just sounded too dorky.

Instead, I just stood up cautiously and looked toward the edge of the lake.

Most of the bees were gone now, some circling the hive, some at the tree. But they weren't swarming angrily around, looking for us anymore.

"Can we go now?" Thomas J said. "My mother will be worried."

"I think so," I said. "I think it's all okay now."

*F*or the next couple days after that Thomas J and I didn't go back to the lake or the tree to find my mood ring, even thought Thomas J kept pestering me that he wanted to get the hive. Instead, we just played around his house or mine. I wasn't chancing anything yet. Who knew about bees? They might stay mad for a long time for all I knew.

I had played at Thomas J's all day Friday, and when I came home it was almost suppertime.

"Is that you, Vada?" Dad yelled down the stairs when I came in.

"Yes," I called back.

"I've been waiting for you," Dad said. "We're going to the fair, the carnival, tonight. Be ready to go in five minutes, okay?"

"Okay!" I shouted. I bounded up the stairs.

Dad popped his head out his bedroom door.

"Shelly's coming with us," he said. "She says you might need a sweater. It gets cold out there at night."

I just stared at him.

Shelly was going? *Shelly* says I need a sweater? What about him and me? He said that night that *we* would go to the fair. He didn't say him and me and *Shelly*.

Dad disappeared back into his room.

"Hurry now," he said.

Why had she ever come here anyway?

And Uncle Phil says Dad's in love with her.

I hated him. Her, too. But what could I do?

When we were all ready and *Shelly* got there, we all got in Dad's car. Of course, I had to sit in the back, and of course I was carsick by the time we got there. I always get carsick sitting in the back, and Dad knows it, too.

As we got out of the car at the fair, Shelly said to me, "Be careful what you eat here. When I was a kid, I went to a carnival with my cousins Gary and Frank. They both ate hot dogs, and next day they got nephritis."

I rolled my eyes. Then I looked straight at Dad. "Nephritis is a kidney disease," I said sweetly. "You don't get it from hot dogs."

Dad just smiled at Shelly and reached out to take her hand.

"Well, I'm no doctor," Shelly said. "Maybe I have the wrong word. But all I know is they both ate hot dogs and they both got this high fever and their faces got very fat."

I looked at Dad again and smiled.

"Well, it's true," Shelly went on. "They baffled medical science. They were in a magazine. *Popular Mechanics*—I mean, *Popular Science.*"

I gave Dad that secret smile again, but he wasn't looking at me. He had an arm around Shelly's shoulder.

"Popular diseases," he whispered to her and they both laughed.

I made a face at their backs.

We left the parking lot and got to the carnival itself. I walked behind.

It was a madhouse, all rides and noise and games. It was hard to even hear yourself think.

There were colored lights swirling on the Ferris wheel and lights on all the zillion other rides. I saw this big ride that looks a little like a spider—a fat body with long legs. At the end of each leg is a cage. The cages sort of get thrown outward from the spider's body while getting spun around and around at the same time.

I hate that ride. Last year I went on it with Thomas J. We were both okay till the ride was over. Then Thomas J stepped off the ride and threw up all over my shoes.

"What's your favorite ride, Vada?" Shelly asked me as we passed the merry-go-round.

"The freak show," I said.

Mean. As mean as I could be.

After that we went on some rides and played some games and mostly it was fun. Although I did get sick of seeing Dad and Shelly making eyes at each other. And

I thought if they whispered to each other even once more, I would definitely throw up.

And then, when we were all very tired and just about to go home, I saw something that really almost made me throw up.

We were trying to get Ping-Pong balls to land in little fish bowls so I could win a fish. It took a zillion throws, but finally I won a fish! Wow! If I could have thrown that good the other day, we would have hit the beehive on the first throw.

"I won! I won!" I said.

They gave me the fish in a little plastic bag of water, and I immediately named it Shelly. It looked just like her, with its big open mouth.

"That's a gorgeous goldfish, Vada," Shelly said, handing the fish to me.

And then that's when I saw Shelly's hand. And the ring. It wasn't a regular ring, like my mood ring or anything. It was a diamond ring. On her left hand. Like an . . . engagement ring.

"Shelly?" I said. "Where'd you get the ring? Did you win it?"

Shelly looked at Dad and took a deep breath.

"Harry, you tell her," she said softly.

"Well, Vada," Dad said. "We have good news. Shelly and I are going to get married."

I dropped my fish. Married. They were going to get married.

"My fish!" I said, and I bent to pick it up. Was my fish all right? I held it up and looked at it.

Married. They were going to get married.

"You'll be okay, little fish," I whispered. *"You* will."

Neither Dad nor Shelly said anything more, like they were waiting. For what?

Finally Shelly sighed. "Vada?" she said quietly. "You okay? You want us to get you another fish?"

"No, he's fine. Fish are very resilient animals, you know." I held the bag up and looked in at it. "Don't worry, fish," I said. "I won't get another fish."

Dad was frowning at me. "Don't we have some things to talk about? Our wedding? Your new mother?"

She'll *never* be my mother. But I didn't say it. I didn't say anything.

After a minute Shelly said, "Look! Bumper cars! How can you go to a carnival without riding the bumper cars?"

"I'll go on them with you!" I said suddenly.

Dad took my fish and Shelly and I went to the bumper cars.

I'm great at bumper cars. Last year I bumped Thomas J till he could hardly stand for a week.

I got my car and steered it straight for Shelly.

She had gotten stuck in a corner, and she had no way out.

I charged her at full speed.

Bam!

She looked surprised.

I rammed her again. And again.

Too bad about her and Dad. Because I did like Shelly.

I just didn't like her and Dad together.

I had her trapped and bammed her a lot more times before she was able to get loose.

She was frowning, looking surprised and—and what? I didn't know. But I thought it was good that she should know how surprise feels. Especially when it wasn't a good surprise, either.

CHAPTER

XVIII

All night long all I could think of was running away, even though it sounded so babyish. Besides, I was pretty sure that wouldn't work. First, where would I go? I could go to Thomas J's, I knew, because his mother would let me stay for a while. But I also knew she'd tell Dad where I was. And I didn't have any money, anyway, even if I could think of a place to go.

I wished I was old enough to marry Mr. Bixler. I'd go there.

I remembered something Thomas J and I had talked about once a year or so ago, right after Gramoo began being weird. I was hating my house, missing Gramoo, and Dad always busy with dead people. And Thomas J, he was mad at his mom. So together we decided we'd run away to Hollywood. We used to watch reruns of "The Brady Bunch" and "The Partridge Family." I said I wanted to live with the Brady

Bunch, and he said he did, too. So we had a big fight because I told him that the Brady Bunch had enough kids, especially if they were getting me, so he had to live with the Partridge Family. He was mad at first, but finally he agreed. We decided that both families seemed like nice kinds of families to have. I've always wanted to be Marcia Brady.

But I knew now that was a dream of a little kid. What could a kid like me do?

Dad was getting married.

He liked Shelly more than me.

And I hated them both.

I got up and went down the hall, looking for Dad, thinking I'd ask him when they were going to do this. Maybe it wouldn't be for a *long* time yet. Maybe years. That would be all right, because by then I'd be old enough to have left home myself.

But Dad wasn't in his room, and when I looked outside, I couldn't see his car, unless it was still in the garage.

I went in the bathroom to pee.

And that's when I saw it. Oh, no! I was bleeding! Dying! The cancer. It had spread.

I could hardly move for a minute. My pants. There was blood. Everywhere.

Oh, God.

I began to feel weak, my head funny, like I was fainting. Oh, God. The blood, it was draining out of me.

"Daddy!" I went out of the bathroom and raced down the hall.

"Daddy!" I called.

He wasn't anywhere.

I ran downstairs, holding the banister, feeling weak and dizzy.

"Daddy? Daddy?"

He wasn't in the hall.

He wasn't in his office.

I ran down the hall to the kitchen–family room, inching slowly, feeling the blood dripping down my legs.

No one was in the kitchen, not even Gramoo.

All the girls talk about getting their period. But this wasn't my period. This was way too much blood. I was hemorrhaging, I knew it.

"Daddy!"

I began crying. I couldn't help it.

I ran back to the hall, just as Shelly was walking in the front door.

"Vada?" she said. "What's wrong?"

"Where's Daddy?"

"He just left. What's the matter?"

"I'm hemorrhaging!"

"What do you mean, hemorrhaging?"

"I want Daddy! I want Gramoo. I don't want you."

I turned to run upstairs, but Shelly came and caught me by the arms.

"Vada?" Shelly turned me to look at her. "Did this happen in the bathroom? Is that what you mean?"

I nodded.

"How old are you, Vada?" Shelly asked.

"I'm eleven and a half," I said.

Shelly sighed. "Come upstairs with me," she said quietly. "We have to have a talk."

"Talk? I'm bleeding to death."

"No. No, you're not," she said. "Come with me. It's okay."

And for some reason, her calm made me feel calm, too.

She took me by the hand like I was just a little kid. And, weird—but I let her.

She led me upstairs and into my room. I sat down on my bed, and she sat down with me.

"Are you going to tell me this is my period?" I said.

She raised her eyebrows. "You know about that?"

I nodded.

"Then why do you think you're hemorrhaging?" she asked.

I shrugged. I couldn't tell her how dumb I really felt about it, that all I knew was what some of the girls whispered about and what the school nurse told us that one time—that it lasted five to seven days—*every* month. And that we couldn't go swimming when we had it. But the nurse never said why about any of it, not even the swimming part.

And she also never told us it would be like this.

It wasn't fair! Why did girls have this? Why not boys?

And right then, when I asked, Shelly told me why. Right then. Everything.

Gross!

I mean, it wasn't news to me or anything, how babies got made, but I never knew about the rest of it, why my period had anything to do with it.

It was disgusting, I decided. Just disgusting. Why

did it have to happen to me? I wasn't ever going to have a baby, anyway.

I got up off the bed. "I think it should be outlawed," I said.

Shelly just smiled. "Vada, it's a very beautiful thing. And look, without it there never would have been a Vada."

"I still think it's disgusting."

"Believe me," Shelly said, "someday you'll feel differently."

Shelly gave me some stuff to use then, and I went in the bathroom.

Gross.

Oh, yuck. I felt like I was wearing a pillow.

And for the rest of my life? Or at least till I was old, maybe forty-five or something?

I couldn't wait to get to be forty-five.

I came back to my room.

Shelly was still waiting for me, sitting on my bed.

"You okay?" she asked.

"No."

"You will be, believe me," she said.

I went to the window and looked out.

I saw Thomas J coming toward my house on his bike. I watched him drop his bike to the ground, and then the bell rang.

"It's Thomas J," I said to Shelly. "I don't want to see him. It's not fair. Nothing happens to boys. Go down and tell him to go away."

"Vada," Shelly said. "It's all right. You can't hide for the rest of your life. Nothing's changed. Go on. Go answer the door. He's your friend."

I just gave her a look.

But she was right—I couldn't just sit in my room all day. Besides, I remembered I was mad at her. I didn't want to stay here with her.

But I wasn't going downstairs, either, not just yet.

I opened the window and stuck my head out. "Thomas J," I called down. "I'm up here. What do you want?"

"Want to do something?" he said, bending his neck back to see me.

"Like what?" I said.

"It's broiling hot out," he said. "We could go to the lake and find your mood ring? Go swimming, maybe?"

Swimming?

"No!" I yelled.

"How come?" He stared up at me. "It's hot!"

"Go away!" I said. "Go away. Go and don't come back for five to seven days!"

And I slammed the window down. Hard.

CHAPTER

XIX

*T*hat was the beginning of the worst two days of my life. All I could think about was what was happening to me, to my body. Think about it and feel it. It felt absolutely gross. I didn't understand how all those girls in my class could get so excited when it happened to them. Unless they were all lying and they all hated it just as much as I did.

I wouldn't even go out. I even missed poetry class. I felt like everyone would know I had it just by looking at me.

But even worse than that—Dad was getting married. And he definitely liked Shelly more than me.

For the next few days I saw him and Shelly sneaking kisses all over the place. And then one night I got in big trouble because I was thinking about them and thinking about everything else that was wrong—so I forgot to lock Gramoo up in the kitchen when people were coming for a viewing.

Big mistake. Because Gramoo got loose and went in there, in the room where there was a viewing going on. I wasn't downstairs when it happened, so I didn't see it. But Dad said she took a rose off the casket and used it like a microphone. And she stood there in front of some dead guy and began singing, booming out in this huge voice, "There's No Business like Show Business." Right there in front of the dead guy and all his live relatives, too.

Actually, I thought it was pretty funny, but Dad was mad as anything. And he blamed it all on me and yelled at me again, right in front of Shelly.

"Do you have any idea how upset those people were?" he shouted. And he put his hands on my shoulders as if he was going to shake me, but then he just dropped his hands. "What were you thinking of?" he growled.

I felt like telling him what I was thinking of. But of course I didn't.

Besides, it wasn't my fault that Gramoo was weird now.

I hated him. If there'd been anywhere to run to, I'd have run.

Instead, next morning early I got on my bike and rode and rode. I rode until lunchtime, then went home and ate, then went out riding again. I rode until I stopped being so mad. Riding my bike helps me think, too, just think quiet thoughts. And I sure had a lot to think about.

Mostly what I thought about was running away. But

it was just too babyish. Because a kid couldn't really get far, especially without any money.

I wondered if there was any way to get kidnapped. I mean, not hurt, just kidnapped for a while. I bet then they'd worry. In social studies, we read about the Lindbergh baby and how someone stole him right out of his bedroom.

Maybe I'd sleep with my window open tonight.

By late afternoon I was tired of riding around, and I went and found Thomas J.

Together we rode to the lake.

We could see the hive still on the ground over by the oak tree, but there weren't any bees around. Still, I wasn't ready to go over there yet, even if my mood ring was still there.

The mood ring could wait. And I told Thomas J he couldn't get the hive, even though he was promising me that it was empty. Well, I wasn't sure it was empty, and I had no intention of having to jump in the lake again. Not now. Let it wait awhile.

Thomas J and I dropped our bikes and went over by the willow tree. We lay on our backs on the grass, staring up at the sky.

There were big fluffy clouds up there, floating along slowly, changing and shifting shapes. I saw an old man with a beard, some dinosaurs, and a frog on a lily pad.

Thomas J said he saw God riding on a horse.

God? How did he know what God looked like?

He just shrugged, and then he laughed. "Well, maybe it isn't God," he said.

I looked at him, and then I laughed, too.

Thomas J is really sweet.

After a while I said, "Thomas J, why do you think people want to get married?"

Thomas J chewed on his blade of grass. "I think when you get old, you just have to, that's all," he said, after a while.

"I'm going to marry Mr. Bixler," I said.

"You can't marry a teacher!" Thomas J said. "It's against the law."

"Is not."

"Is, too. There's some rule. Besides, suppose you did? He'd have to give you all A's, and it wouldn't be fair."

"Dummy!" I said. "I'm not going to marry him *yet*. I meant when I grow up."

"What if he doesn't wait for you?" Thomas J said.

I just shrugged. He'd wait. I knew.

I sighed. "And know what else?" I said. "My dad gave Shelly a ring."

"A ring?" Thomas J got up on an elbow and looked at me. "What kind? A mood ring?"

"Not a mood ring," I said. "An engagement ring."

"They're getting married?"

I nodded.

"Wow!" Thomas J said. He lay back down on the ground. "Wow! Then you'll get to have a mother, too."

He sounded super-pleased.

"Well, I don't like her," I said.

"I do," Thomas J said. "She's real funny."

"Yeah. Well, he likes her better than he likes me," I said, so quietly I could hardly hear myself.

"What?" Thomas J said.

"Nothing," I said.

We were quiet awhile, and then I asked, "Thomas J? Have you ever kissed anyone?"

"My mother."

I poked him with my elbow—hard.

"I didn't mean that!"

He laughed. "I know. You mean like they do on TV." He shook his head. "No."

I rolled over on my stomach so he wouldn't see my face. I pulled up some grass. "Maybe we should," I said. "Just to see what's the big deal."

"I don't know," Thomas J said. He sounded nervous. "I don't think so."

"Here," I said. "Practice on your arm. Like this."

I started kissing my arm, pressing my lips hard against it, making noises like they do on TV.

After a minute Thomas J did the same.

We both stopped at the same time.

"Okay," I said. "Enough practice. Close your eyes."

He slid backwards on his elbows across the grass, away from me.

"Why?" he said. "I won't be able to see."

"Just *do* it!" I said.

I followed him across the grass, leaning over him till my face was right above his.

Thomas J closed his eyes. But even with his eyes closed, I could tell he was nervous, the way his eyelids were twitching.

"Okay," I said. "On the count of three. One . . . two . . . two and a half . . . three . . ."

I closed my eyes, too, then bent over and kissed him right on the lips.

He kissed back. Like, really pressed his lips on mine hard.

It felt like . . . It felt like . . .

I pulled away from him.

It felt . . . Wow.

Thomas J was looking right at me, very surprised, like.

It was very quiet, only the cicadas singing in the trees.

It was *really* quiet.

"Say something," I said.

He swallowed hard. "Um . . . Um . . ."

"Hurry!" I said.

He jumped to his feet. "I pledge allegiance to the flag of the United States of America," he said.

He put his hand over his heart. "And to the Republic for which it stands, one nation, under God, indivisible, with liberty and justice for all."

Dummy!

But both of us were hysterical by the time he finished. And relieved, too. Relieved of what, I had no idea, but I definitely felt relieved when we were laughing like that.

After that we stayed there at the lake for a long time, mostly being stupid, making up dumb jokes and pushing each other around and stuff. After a while Thomas J wanted to go find my mood ring, but I told him no way. Not with me around, anyway. Like I told him, I had no intention of having to jump in the lake again—not now.

Finally when it was beginning to get dark and Thomas J said he was hungry, we got up and started for home.

As we turned onto our street, I said to him, "Don't you dare tell anybody."

"Yeah, well, you better not, either," he said.

"I won't," I said. "You won't?"

"Promise," Thomas J said. And then he added, "Spit on it?"

But I knew he was joking. It's something we did when we were very little—spit in our hands and then shook hands.

Yuck.

"See you tomorrow?" I said.

"All right. See you," Thomas J said.

I headed for my house, and Thomas J headed for his. But after just a minute, I heard him yelling for me.

"Vada!"

I stopped. "What?"

"Would you . . ." But he didn't say any more.

I turned and saw him facing me, but not exactly looking at me, his chin tucked down into his chest, kind of shy-looking.

"Would I what?" I said.

He poked at the ground with his sneaker. "Would you . . . think of me?" he said.

"Think of you?" I said. "For what?"

"You know," he said. "Like . . . like if you don't get to marry Mr. Bixler?"

I smiled. Yeah. Yeah, I would. I definitely would.

"Okay," I said. "I guess."

I turned and raced for home. I didn't want him to see how I was smiling.

CHAPTER

XX

*N*ext morning I lay in bed awhile thinking, sort of daydreaming. Weird, how days change. Just a few days ago, I was so miserable. I'd gotten my period, Dad was getting married, and nobody loved me anymore. Today . . . well, not much had changed, but I didn't feel so sad anymore. I was still mad at Dad, and I still surely didn't want him to get married. But something strange had happened to me.

Maybe it was Thomas J. Maybe it was just growing up. And maybe . . . well, maybe growing up wouldn't be as terrible as I had thought.

I even started to write a poem about it, about growing up. I wasn't sure I'd want to read it in class next week. But I might.

I lay for a while thinking about it, then got up and put on shorts and a shirt. I'd get Thomas J, and we'd do something. Maybe it would be safe to go find my mood ring by now.

I heard the doorbell ring and opened my door, thinking maybe it was Thomas J already. But it was grown-up voices, Dad's and somebody else's—a man. Probably somebody wanting to bring in more dead people, so I shut the door again.

I was hungry and ready to go down for breakfast when I remembered something.

My fish! My poor fish.

I kept forgetting to feed him. Yesterday I hadn't fed him anything.

I went over to his bowl and looked in. He wasn't floating on top or gasping or anything, although the water was pretty scummy-looking. I'd change it later.

But not now. I just got the fish food and shook a whole bunch into the water.

There. That should make up for forgetting to feed him yesterday.

I was just finishing, when there was a knock and Dad opened my door.

"Vada?" he said. "Can I come in?"

"Yeah," I said.

But he was already in.

He came over to where I was standing and looked in the fishbowl. But he didn't say a word.

What was he up to? Was he going to apologize for yelling at me the other night? He should, anyway. Or maybe he was going to tell me that he and Shelly weren't getting married after all?

He opened his mouth and then closed it a few times. And finally he said, "What are you doing?"

"Feeding my fish," I said.

"Is that the fish you won at the carnival?" he said.

I sighed. Gosh. How many fish did he think I had? He knew I'd never had one before.

"He's getting big," Dad said, still looking down into the bowl.

I leaned against the windowsill and folded my arms. Right. Dad had come in to tell me my fish was getting big. And I'd only had it about a week.

I wanted to say, Dad, just get to the point. But I didn't.

Because just then he looked at me. Uh-oh. Something was wrong. Something about his face made me very, very nervous.

And then I knew. He was going to tell me that he and Shelly had decided to get married right away. Now. Today, I bet. Or maybe they were married already? Maybe that's what he was going to tell me?

"Vada," Dad said, turning away and going to sit on my bed. "Come sit next to me."

He sat down and patted the place beside him.

I didn't move.

"Come on," he said. And then he added, "Please." And his voice sounded weird, choked up or something, the way mine did when I was trying not to cry.

Something was coming. Something was coming. And I wasn't going to like it.

I went and sat next to him, my heart pounding hard.

"Vada," Dad said. He stopped and put both hands over his face, then straightened up, cleared his throat, and started again. "Vada, something's happened to Thomas J. He stepped on a beehive last night."

I shook my head. "That dummy! I told him not to tease those bees. And I told him to leave that hive alone. Did he get stung?"

Dad nodded. "Yes," he said. He swallowed. "Yes, he did."

I stood up. "Maybe I should go over and yell at him," I said.

"No, sweetheart," Dad said. He quick reached up and took my hands, holding them tight. "Don't do that. You can't."

"Can't? What do you mean, can't?" I pulled my hands loose. "I'll go do it now."

Dad just shook his head, his face weird—hurt—sad, maybe, like somebody had just hurt his feelings.

Suddenly something terrible began happening inside my chest. But all I said was "Sure I can. Sure."

Dad was still shaking his head.

"Why not?" I said. "Why can't I?"

"He was allergic to bees," Dad said, so softly.

"Oh, him!" I laughed—tried to laugh. "He's allergic to everything," I said. "Right? You know what? He's even allergic to chocolate. And you know what else? Last year . . ."

But Dad was just shaking his head, hard.

The lump was huge inside my throat.

I swallowed hard. "Dad?" I said. "Dad, he's all right, isn't he?"

Dad shook his head again. And then he looked up at me. And . . . but . . . he couldn't be. Dad was—crying? *Dad* was crying?

"Dad?" I practically shouted it. I was shaking so I couldn't stand it. *"Dad?"*

Dad stood up and took both my hands in his again, holding them hard. "There were just too many of them, Vada," he said. "I'm sorry, sweetheart."

I pulled away from him. "Too many what?" I said, my throat so tight it would surely burst. "Too many *what?*"

"Bees. Too many bees. Thomas J is dead. He's dead, Vada."

"No!" I said. "No! You liar!"

Dead. Dead. Dead. Dead, he's dead, Vada.

And then he tried pulling me close.

"Don't touch me!" I yanked away from his hands. "Don't touch me, you liar! Children don't die! You said those coffins weren't for children."

"Vada, please," Dad said. "Please, baby."

"No!"

I wanted to get out of there, out of that room, but he was blocking the way.

I backed up to the wall, Dad following me.

"Please, Vada."

"No!"

I was up against the shelf. The fishbowl. The fish food.

I snatched up the fish food, then turned and flung it at Dad. Hard.

The food flew all over the place, all over the floor, all over Dad.

"Get out!" I shouted. "Get out! I hate you! You liar!"

"Vada, please."

I turned away. What? What to do? Why was he lying to me like this?

"No!" I said. "No!"

Not Thomas J.

He *was* lying.

Not Thomas J. Thomas J is my friend.

Everyone dies.

Not Thomas J. No.

I picked up the fishbowl. Turned.

And dumped it over, all over Dad's shoes, all over the floor. Fish and all.

My fish would die! Right there on the floor.

I ducked under Dad's arms and ran from the room.

My fish was dead. I had killed it. My fish was dead.

I ran downstairs and out of the house.

Where? Where to go?

My throat. It hurt so. I was choking. It hurt.

Dr. Welty! Dr. Welty.

But where was my bike?

I couldn't find my bike.

In the garage. The phrenology skull. Ha, Thomas J, you have no personality. None!

Yeah? Show me where it says that.

To Dr. Welty's.

No bike. I ran, ran all the way.

I ran up the steps, into the waiting room. Dr. Welty was there at the desk, talking to Mrs. Randall.

My throat. I couldn't stand the pain. I reached out as Dr. Welty turned to me.

"Vada!" he said. "Vada, what's wrong?"

"I can't breathe," I said. I was gasping, holding my throat. "I'm suffocating. Help me."

He came to me and picked me up—picked me up.

He carried me into the examining room and laid me on the table.

"It's all right," he said. He kept on saying, "It's all right. It's all right. Take deep breaths. Come on, it's all right. Hush, hush, now."

"It hurts, it hurts so bad. Please make it stop. Please!"

"What hurts, Vada?" he said quietly. "Breathe slowly and talk to me. What hurts?"

"The bee stings. The bee stings. I can't breathe. Oh, God, it hurts. It hurts so bad."

CHAPTER

XXI

I went to the lake after that. There was nothing else to do. Nobody to do it with. Dr. Welty wanted me to wait for Dad to come get me, but I told him I had to walk. I'd go home, I said. But first, I went to the lake. At the lake, I climbed up in the willow tree and sat for a long time staring out at the water.

Then, I did something I'd never done before: I stood up, climbed higher, and found an almost bare branch near the top of the tree. I pulled myself to a standing position, and began walking the branch like a tightrope walker.

I took four . . . five . . . six steps.

Thomas J. He'd be so . . .

So what?

And then I slipped and crashed down several branches before I caught myself. My heart was beating wildly.

And then, very calmly, I climbed down and headed for home.

There was nowhere else to go, anyway. Nothing to do. No one to do it with.

Thomas J. He wasn't dead. He couldn't be. I knew he wasn't. They were lying.

We played together just yesterday.

I told him I'd . . . I'd think of him if I didn't get to marry Mr. Bixler.

I promised him.

He was my brother. My blood brother.

Home.

I walked home.

Thomas J.

Thomas J? You jerk.

You went back to the beehive. I told you not to.

Dork. Jerk. Retard. What'd you do that for? Collecting beehives. You *are* weird, just like everybody says.

I'll come over later and see you. I will.

Dad lied.

Children don't die. He said so himself. You'll be okay later. Then we'll ride our bikes. Maybe even— maybe even we'll try that, like what we did yesterday —you know, with the kiss?

You better not have told. Better have kept your promise.

You better or I'll kill you. I'll beat you up. You know I can do it, too. I'll sit on your back and bounce— hard, just like I did the other day.

Allergic! You baby.

You're even allergic to *chocolate!*

And *nobody's* allergic to chocolate. Even Shelly said that.

Should I go to Thomas J's?

Where was I?

I looked around me. I was home. In front of my house. There was my bike. How come I hadn't seen it before?

Where was Thomas J's bike?

It was so quiet. Only cicadas in the trees. The sprinkler dropping water on the grass.

I opened the front door and went in, passing Shelly on the stairs.

"Vada?" she said and she reached for me, but I was too fast for her.

I ducked away from her hands and ran to my room, then closed and locked my door.

I had to talk to Thomas J.

Somebody had cleaned up my floor. The fish and the food and the bowl and everything, all were gone.

Where was my fish?

Where was it?

Did he die?

He was too young to die. Children don't die.

Where was Thomas J?

I stayed in my room all day, not talking to anyone, not seeing anyone. I didn't even come out for meals, just to go to the bathroom once in a while.

Shelly knocked on my door lots of times and tried to come in, but I had locked it. And when Shelly wasn't knocking, Dad was. Even Uncle Phil came and knocked once, asking if I wouldn't come down. But I wouldn't talk to them. I couldn't talk to them.

They were lying, both of them. All of them.

And if they brought Thomas J here for a— Well, they *couldn't* bring Thomas J here. Could they?

Oh, God, please.

It hurt, it hurt so bad.

I couldn't breathe again.

I remembered what Dr. Welty said: take deep breaths, it would be all right.

But it wouldn't be all right. It wasn't.

I lay down on my bed, carefully. Something would break if I wasn't careful.

Careful.

It got to be dark, and still I didn't come out of my room.

They were going to bring Thomas J here. I knew it. It was the only place. But they couldn't.

They couldn't bring him in here! He was *scared* of this place. Didn't they know that? And he was scared of the dark, too.

Food. I was hungry. That was it.

If I ate, just like I always did. . . .

Shelly had asked me before, begged me, practically, to come down for dinner. And when I didn't answer, she said she'd leave some food for me outside my door.

I went out in the hall and got the tray and brought it in.

Milk. An apple and raisins. And sandwiches, my favorite—chicken on rye. With tomatoes.

Thomas J's allergic to tomatoes.

I took the tomatoes off and ate some of the chicken part.

But I wasn't really hungry after all.

I don't know how much time went by. It got to be night, and I heard people talking. And I heard— Was it Thomas J's mother talking?

I ran over to the door and opened it softly, listening. It *was* Mrs. Sennett.

I wanted to run down and see if Thomas J was with her. But I didn't. I knew he would never come in here, not in this house. He must have been waiting on the porch.

I'd go down and talk to him. Later.

I closed my door, then went and lay down on my bed.

I must have fallen asleep, because I was awakened by someone talking to me.

I sat up. The room was completely dark, but someone *was* talking. Shelly. And I wasn't dreaming.

But I hadn't unlocked the door. She couldn't be in here.

And then I realized she was outside, right outside my door, talking to me through the door.

"Vada? Vada?" she was saying.

I didn't answer. I wasn't talking to anyone. Only to Thomas J when he got better. After that, I'd talk to Shelly and Dad, too.

"Vada?" Shelly said. "Please come down, sweetie? Please. Don't you want to come down? It's been a whole day. You have to do something. You have to come out. Please?"

I don't have to do anything. Not anything. No.

"Vada? Maybe you should come down for the funeral? It's tomorrow. Sometimes it helps to go to the funeral."

She waited, like waiting for an answer.

Helps? Helps what? Ha!

"Vada?" she began again. "Vada, I want to tell you something. And if you won't let me in, I'll tell you from here. You have a family here. You do. They care. You know, you have your dad and Uncle Phil and Gramoo. I know Gramoo isn't well, but if she could talk, she'd tell you how much she cares. And you know what else? Your dad cares a lot. He just doesn't know what to say. And, Vada, you have me."

I don't want you.

No.

"Vada?" she said again, softly, almost whispering. "You know, Vada, when I first came here, I wasn't crazy about the idea of working with dead people. But when I saw that a family lived here, I thought that if I'm living without a family, at least I could work with one, and maybe once in a while be invited for supper. And then . . . then we became a family, or we're going to be. . . . Vada, there's nothing like family. Come out, please. So we can help?"

You help? You? You're not my family.

And how come Dad doesn't know what to say? He knows what to say to everyone else. People bring in dead people all the time. He knows just what to say to them.

I sat listening for a long while after that, but she didn't say anything more. I sort of hoped she would.

But it was quiet for a long time. And then I think she went away.

When next I woke up it was light out and I could hear people walking around and talking downstairs.

I got up and looked out the window.

There was a hearse out there. So they must be going to have a funeral today. It was a big hearse, though, big enough to carry a grown-up coffin, so it wasn't for Thomas J. It would have been a little one. For children.

No.

I saw people coming up the walk to the house— Reverend Miles and Mrs. Miles, both of them wearing black.

Stupid.

Thomas J hates black.

I could hear people talking, hear Dad greeting people. And then it got very, very quiet.

I pressed my ear to the door, listening.

But the only sound was Reverend Miles talking, droning on and on like he does in church when he puts Dad to sleep. Was he praying? Thomas J prays, I know he does. We've talked about it lots of times.

"There are no words that I could say," Reverend Miles was saying, "that could begin to express the loss and grief we feel for our beloved Thomas."

Beloved.

Where was he now? Were there really horses for him to ride in heaven? Would he be able to ride? And what if he was allergic to them?

I could still hear Reverend Miles. "One word that must keep going through our heads is—why?" he said. "Why would God take this little boy from us?"

Why? Why?

I could come out. Dad and Shelly would be down there listening to Reverend Miles. They wouldn't see me if I came out.

Quietly I opened my door a crack. I tiptoed from my door to the top of the stairs. Very quietly I crouched on the top step.

I could hear Reverend Miles clearly now.

"There are no clear answers," he was saying, "but there is comfort in knowing he is cared for."

Cared for? By whom? What if he's scared up there? What if the horses don't have wings and he falls? I was just making that up, about the clouds. What if I was wrong, and the clouds don't hold him up? Who will take care of him? Who will bully him and make him not afraid, like I always did?

"So while I can't give you an answer to 'why?'" Reverend Miles went on, "I can tell you that God has chosen Thomas for some very special purpose."

What purpose?

I went a little farther down the steps, but not so far that I could see inside that room, that viewing room. I didn't want to see inside that room. No.

I just wanted to . . . be closer, maybe.

"And we must find solace in knowing that Thomas is now in God's care," Reverend Miles said. "And now I would like to read a passage from the Bible and hope it will be of some comfort. Turn with me to Matthew nineteen, verse thirteen.

In *God's* care?

I don't want him in God's care. I want Thomas J *here!*

Quietly I slipped inside the door of the viewing room and looked quickly around.

They were all bent over their Bibles, looking for the place, and no one saw me.

I didn't want to look where he was—there in the front corner of the room where they always have the coffins.

The child's coffin.

I didn't want to look. But I did. I had to.

Slowly I went over to him.

Thomas J!

I bent over him. "Your face is so puffy!" I whispered. "Oh, God, it must hurt so! It's so puffy. Damn bees!"

I stepped back.

"You dummy!" I whispered. "I *told* you not to bother them."

Reverend Miles was praying again.

". . . And children were brought to him so that he could place his hands on them in prayer. The disciples began to scold them, but Jesus said, 'Let the children come to me. Do not hinder them. . . .'"

I bent close to Thomas J again. "Come on with me, Thomas J," I whispered to him. "Let's go climb trees. We'll go to the willow tree."

He didn't move, didn't . . .

I reached out to touch him. "Your face," I whispered. "Does it hurt real bad?"

Suddenly it was very quiet. No one was praying. And Dad and Shelly were standing there by me.

"Vada," Dad said softly.

I turned to him. "I have to get Thomas J to come with me," I said.

I turned back. "Come on, Thomas J," I said.

"Vada!" Dad said.

And then I noticed something—Thomas J! His glasses. He didn't have on his glasses.

I turned back to Dad. "Where's his glasses?" I said. "Get his glasses. He can't see without them. Put his glasses on! Now!"

Dad took me in his arms, held my face against his chest. "Vada!" he whispered. "Vada, he's gone!"

I looked up at him.

It was very quiet in the room.

"He was going to be an acrobat," I said.

Dad let go of me.

"Please, sweetheart," Dad said.

I backed away from him. "No," I said. I shook my head. "No. No."

I raced out of there, down the street.

Thomas J was dead. He was.

I turned once, and Dad was following me, but then, when I looked around again he was gone.

I turned the corner, not knowing where I was going—and almost ran right into Mr. Bixler's arms, Mr. Bixler with some woman, both of them coming down the steps of that house he was fixing up.

"Vada!" he said, holding my arms and crouching down so he was looking right in my face. "Are you all right? I was just coming over to your house. I'm so sorry about Thomas J."

I thought of what Gramoo says. Sing. Sing.

"Blitie blop, bloopie, you twinkle above us, we twinkle. . . ." I sang.

"Okay, Vada!" Mr. Bixler said, still holding my arms. "We don't have to talk about him if you don't want."

I stopped singing and pulled away from him.

We were all quiet. That lady with him looked like she was crying.

After a minute I said, "Justin and Ronda said I should say what I feel."

"Yes," Mr. Bixler said.

I looked at my shoes.

"Mr. Bixler," I said, "I love you."

I looked up, and he was staring at me, wide-eyed. Surprised.

Was it a good surprise or a bad one?

"I love you the way my dad loves Shelly," I said. "And I want to live here with you."

"Vada, I think your father would miss you," he said. "He would, a lot."

"No, he wouldn't," I said. "And I can't go home."

The woman with Mr. Bixler suddenly took his hand. Tears were running down her face.

"Who's she?" I said.

"Vada," Mr. Bixler said. "This is Suzanne." He hesitated. "We're getting married in the fall."

"I'm so sorry about Thomas J, Vada," Suzanne said.

I just stared at her. At him. Getting *married*.

Then he wasn't getting a pet.

"Vada," Mr. Bixler said. "I was going to bring her to class next week. I wanted her to hear your poems."

I backed up.

"I cared for him, too, Vada," Mr. Bixler said. "Don't go! Let me take you home."

But I was already gone.

Out of there.

Nowhere.

Nowhere to go. Nobody to go with.

I ran to the lake, to the willow tree.

I climbed up.

I would stay here. For how long. I didn't know how long I'd stay. Maybe forever. Maybe for life.

Maybe till I died.

Because I was going to die now. Not from that thing

in my throat. That was nothing now. I was dying from something else.

I didn't know what to call it. It wasn't a cancer. But I knew where it was—or actually, where it wasn't. It was right there—something was gone right there, right inside my chest.

CHAPTER

XXIII

I stayed up in the willow tree for a long time, a long, long time.

It got dark, and the moon came out, and I could hear bullfrogs calling and a fish splash in the water. And still I sat. I only got down and went home because I didn't know what else to do, where else to go. I was surprised that I was still alive, that the hole in my chest hadn't made me die yet.

Thomas J was dead. And he's my best friend.

But I was alive. And I didn't know what else to do but go home.

When I came up the steps, it was already pitch dark. The hearse was gone, but there was a police car by the door.

When I went up onto the porch, I could hear the policeman and Shelly inside.

"But you *have* to find her!" Shelly was saying.

169

"It's getting dark, and she can't be alone in the dark."

"We'll keep looking," the policeman said.

"We've been out all day trying to find her. Her father's out there now. Her teacher called this afternoon. She went there first."

"Yes, you told us, ma'am."

"But I can't just sit here. She's only eleven years old, and her only friend in the world is dead. I should . . ."

I don't know what she thought she should do.

Because I walked in then right past them. Or tried to.

Shelly grabbed me by the arms and hugged me to her, rocking me, rocking me. I didn't pull away.

I was tired.

"Vada, Vada, where have you been? We've been worried sick about you, sweetie." She hugged me so tight it almost hurt, then held me away and looked me over. "Are you all right?"

I nodded.

No.

"Thank God," Shelly said, and she hugged me again.

"Glad everything's all right," the policeman said. And I heard him go down the steps.

I went upstairs to my room, and Shelly followed me up.

I went in the bathroom, and she followed me in there. She washed my hands and face and stayed there while I peed and brushed my teeth. Then she went with me back to my room, where she undressed me and helped me into my pajamas, just like I was about three years old.

I let her. It was okay. I was too tired to do anything else.

When I was all ready, I got into bed and Shelly tucked me in. She fixed the covers all the way around, almost as if it was wintertime.

That was all right, too. I didn't care.

When I was all tucked in, Shelly sat down next to me on the bed and smoothed my hair back from my face.

"Vada," she said, "your dad was so upset. He really does love you very much. It's just that some people have trouble saying how they feel."

"I told Mr. Bixler that I love him," I said.

"That's good, good that you say that."

"But he didn't like me."

"Of course he likes you. Someday, believe me, someone will feel about you the same way you feel about them. And it'll make you so happy. And it *will* happen to you."

"I should have told Thomas J that he was my best friend. He told me that the other day. And I didn't tell him back."

"I bet he knew."

I didn't say anything for a while. I didn't know if I could say what I had to say, but I knew I had to try. Nothing mattered much anymore anyway. "Shelly?"

"Yes, sweetie?"

"I stole your money from the cookie jar to take the writing class."

"Oh, sweetie. It's all right."

"I'll pay you back," I said.

She bent and kissed my head, then kept her face pressed into my hair. "You just dedicate your first book to me," she whispered, "and I'll forget the whole thing."

I shook my head. "I don't think I'll ever go back to writing class."

"You will. Someday. And then I get the book dedicated to me, okay?"

"If I ever write one, I will," I said.

I fell asleep, right then with Shelly still sitting on my bed, still smoothing my hair. But when I woke up next, no one was in the room with me. But I woke because I heard Dad downstairs.

"Is she here?" he said. And then I heard him say, "Thank God!"

And then I heard him run upstairs, and he opened my door, and the light from the hall crept across the floor.

I heard him come to stand beside the bed.

But for some reason I couldn't look up at him.

He stood there for a long time, so long that I thought maybe he was gone. But then he bent and kissed me, softly on my forehead. And I heard him going out of the room.

I had to know. Had to. And nothing worse could happen anyway, nothing more than what had happened already.

"Dad?" I said. "Did I kill my mother?"

Dad turned abruptly. "What?" he said.

I sat up in bed. "The bees killed Thomas J. And I killed my mother."

Dad came back to my bed and sat beside me. He pulled me close. "No, no, Vada, it just happened. It wasn't your fault. How can it be a baby's fault?"

"I found this," I said.

I dug under the pillow and pulled out the picture I had found in the garage the other day.

Dad held it up so he could see it in the light from the hall. "I forgot about this picture," he said, smiling. "Where'd you find it?"

"In the garage."

"That was her favorite car," Dad said.

"What was my mother like?"

"What was she like?" Dad said. "Oh, she was pretty, like you. And she was kind. And you have her eyes. And boy, did she love to laugh." He put the picture down and stroked my hair. "Sometimes when you laugh, you sound just like her."

"Do I?"

"Uh-huh."

When I laugh, I sound like her.

There was a long pause, and then Dad said, "When she found out she was going to have you, you know what she did?"

I shook my head no.

"She came home and started painting your room pink. She was sure she was going to have a little girl."

"Did she want a girl?"

Me?

"Yes. Yes, she did."

"Did you—do you—miss her?"

"Yes, I did. For a long time. And even now I sometimes get sad when I see a pretty flower—dahlias were her favorites—or when I see one of those purple sunsets and know that your mother would have liked it. And those perfect summer or winter nights when the stars seem to come right down to the horizon. She loved beautiful things." He stroked my hair. "She would have loved you."

"I think that every time I see a weeping willow tree or those empty cicada shells, I'll think of Thomas J."

Suddenly Dad hugged me, hugged me so fiercely that for a moment I could hardly breathe.

But I didn't hug him back.

"I'm sorry, Vada," Dad said, and I could tell that he was crying. "I haven't helped you much. See, I wanted to keep you from it, but I just couldn't. At first I thought—what could I say to you? See, day after day people come to me when their family dies. They bring fathers, mothers. And even their children. And they all look to me to make things better. But all I can offer are a few nice words. I wanted to do more than that for you. I wanted it to never happen to you. I even lied to you. I told you . . . that children don't die. Of course you knew. But . . . I wanted to protect you. And I couldn't. I didn't know how. I *don't* know how."

He was still hugging me, holding me close. And then, little by little, I found myself hugging him back.

I even patted his shoulder and his back a little, the way Gramoo used to do to me.

"I still don't know how to help you," Dad said. "I can't make it better."

Dad's arms were tight around me, his shoulder warm and close.

And I found I was crying again. Crying. But . . .

Dad brought my head down to his chest, rocking me a little. "Vada," he said, "I know that Thomas J never came in here, and I know why, too. He was afraid of this place. I understand. I was born in this house. I remember my eighth birthday. My mother planned a huge party for me."

"Gramoo?"

"Gramoo. And she invited all my friends, but not one of them showed up. They were all afraid to." He held me away and looked down at me. "I think I know how you feel—must have felt—with Thomas J afraid of this house."

For a long time Daddy continued to hold me in his arms, rocking me like I was just a little baby. It was almost like he had forgotten I was grown up.

I don't think he'd held me for that long since I was four.

"You know," he said softly after a while, "I must have seen hundreds of funerals in this house. When it's an old person, you say, Well, they had a wonderful life. But when it's . . . someone eleven years old, I don't know what to say. I don't know how to help you, so I haven't said much. But I know that was a mistake. I can't make it better but . . ."

His shoulders were shaking, and I could feel his breath all trembly. "I'm sorry," he said. "It's not that

I don't care. It's just that I can't make it better. And I want to."

No. He couldn't make it better. Well.

Dad straightened up then, and hugged me once more. Then, very gently, he laid me back down on the pillow. "You're a good girl," he said softly. "And I want you to be happy. Don't be like me."

He kissed my head, then laid his hand against my forehead.

"How's your throat?" he said. "Maybe you should go see Dr. Welty?"

"No," I said. "It's nothing."

Dad got up and went to the door.

"Daddy?" I said.

He stopped.

"Daddy," I said, "it's not so bad to be like you."

Summer is almost over now, and it's been bad—really bad. But sometimes I make it better by playing games with myself, making believe Thomas J is just away, like maybe at summer camp. And Shelly helps, too, by doing stuff with me, and so does Dad. Dad helps by just talking to me. It's like we understand each other a little better now.

And it's not all bad. I am writing. Judy's going to be in my homeroom in the fall. And Dad and Shelly are going to get married.

I think I might like that now. I don't think it's going to be too bad. Like Thomas J said, now I'll get to have a mother, too.

Gramoo is still weird and not going to get better. And Uncle Phil . . . well, he's just the same. But I haven't been back to see Dr. Welty all summer practically.

It was the last week of the writing class, and I hadn't been back there, either, not since Thomas J died.

But I had written a poem for Thomas J one day, and I wanted to read it to the class, to Mr. Bixler, especially. So I got dressed up, in a dress, just like a grown-up, and went to the class.

They were meeting out in that courtyard again, sitting in a circle on the grass. I was purposely late. I didn't want to stay, either, just wanted to read my poem and go home.

Mr. Bixler was reading as I came in. He stopped short and looked at me.

Everyone turned.

"I was hoping you'd come by," Mr. Bixler said.

"Hey, welcome back, man!" Justin said.

"I can't stay," I said. "I just came to read my poem."

"We'd love to hear it," Mr. Bixler said.

Everyone looked at me.

I was still standing, and I stayed there, and I read: "Weeping willow, with your tears running down, why do you always weep and frown? Is it because he left you one day? Is it because he could not stay? On your branches he would swing. Do you long for the happiness that day would bring? He found shelter in your shade. You thought his laughter would never fade. Weeping willow, stop your tears, for there is something to calm your fears. You think death has ripped you forever apart. But I know he'll always be in your heart."

I looked up. "That's all," I said.

Nobody said anything, not even that it was nice.

But I saw lots of people take out handkerchiefs and wipe their eyes.

Justin gave me the peace sign. And Mr. Bixler, he had tears in his eyes that he wasn't even trying to hide.

I went outside then.

The sun was shining through the trees, but it was slanty in the sky, a fading kind of weak light now. Fall was definitely coming on.

I wondered what it was like where Thomas J was, whether there really were horses with wings in heaven and you fell into soft clouds. . . .

I walked on home, but just as I came up on the porch, the door opened, and Dad and Mrs. Sennett, Thomas J's mother, came out.

I didn't want to see her. But there she was, and I couldn't avoid her now.

"Vada," Mrs. Sennett said.

"Hello, Mrs. Sennett," I said.

She held out her hand. "I wanted to give this to you. Thomas J had this on him when . . . He was holding this and the beehive that day. I thought you might like to have it."

She put something in my hand.

I looked down at it. It was upside down in my hand, the stone side down. But I knew what it was—my ring, my mood ring.

He had remembered! When he went back for the beehive, he'd remembered my ring!

I looked up at her. At Daddy, standing watching us. I didn't know what to do, what to say.

I missed him more than I had all summer!

I could feel tears welling up in my eyes again.

Mrs. Sennett saw, I know.

"You were such a good friend to him," she said. "I hope you'll still come by and visit me."

I couldn't speak. So I just nodded. I will. A promise.

Daddy came over and put an arm around my shoulders.

Mrs. Sennett went on down the steps and out to the sidewalk.

I looked down at the ring in my hand, then slowly turned it over.

It wasn't black anymore. It was blue. Sky blue!

Sky blue!

Thomas J. Suddenly . . . suddenly I knew where he was.

I ran down the steps.

"Mrs. Sennett!" I called.

She turned back to me.

"Thomas J will be all right!" I said. "He will. My mother will take care of him."

About the Author

PATRICIA HERMES is the author of many highly acclaimed novels for children and young adults. Among her many awards are the California Young Reader Medal, the Pine Tree Book Award and the Hawaii Nene award. Her books have also been named IRA/CBC Children's Choices and Notable Children's Trade Books in the field of Social Studies. Her books have been praised for their "recognizable vitality" (Kirkus Reviews) and "rhythmic, homey text and genuine characters [that] resonate with authenticity" (School Library Journal starred review).

Minstrel Books publishes *Kevin Corbett Eats Flies; Heads, I Win;* and *I Hate Being Gifted.* Archway Paperbacks publishes *Be Still My Heart* and *My Girl.*

Born and educated in New York, Patricia Hermes has taught English at the High School and Junior High level and has taught Gifted and Talented programs in the grade schools. She travels frequently throughout the country, speaking at schools and conferences, to students, teachers, educators, and parents.

The mother of five children, she lives and works in New England.